P9-BXW-678

Goldfish
TN Luu   166652

DATE DUE			—

NEW YORK

SQUARE
FISH

An imprint of Macmillan Publishing Group, LLC
175 Fifth Avenue
New York, NY 10010
fiercereads.com

Printed in the United States of America by LSC Communications, Harrisonburg, Virginia.
Square Fish and the Square Fish logo are trademarks of Macmillan and are used by
Feiwel and Friends under license from Macmillan.

Our books may be purchased in bulk for promotional, educational, or business use.
Please contact your local bookseller or the Macmillan Corporate and
Premium Sales Department at (800) 221-7945 ext. 5442 or by e-mail at
MacmillanSpecialMarkets@macmillan.com.

Library of Congress Cataloging-in-Publication Data Available

ISBN 9781250158406 (paperback)   ISBN 9781250089199 (ebook)

Originally published in the United States by Feiwel and Friends
First Square Fish edition, 2018
Book designed by Anna Booth
Square Fish logo designed by Filomena Tuosto

1   3   5   7   9   10   8   6   4   2

LEXILE: 730L

For Diarmuid

the end

You'd think it would feel weird being nearly naked in front of so many people, but it doesn't.

I ping my swimsuit straps for luck, once right, twice left, walk out poolside, and take a deep breath, inhaling the familiar tang of chlorine and feet. It sounds gross, but that smell is so exciting. I'm where I belong.

I'm one of the fastest swimmers in my county. That's why I'm here—trying out for a High Performance Training Camp that will set me on my way to Team Great Britain. I've wanted this for as long as I can remember. So . . . you know, no pressure, not a big deal, whev.

I think I'm sweating inside my ears.

I pad along the side of the pool, watching the heat before mine. Older swimmers power up and down; they look so strong—they're not so much swimming as punching their way through water.

We're all in a vast glass room. I want to use the word *palace*. It's a palace made of glass, filled with four Olympic-sized swimming pools! It's basically my dream home. The sounds of splashing and shouting bounce off the concrete walls. Ninety percent of the people in this room are having the most important day of their lives.

I look around for my best friend, Hannah, and spot her by the changing room. I give her a quick smile. I think she feels a bit queasy, because she does an elaborate mime of puking into the pool. An official eyes her disapprovingly.

I know how she feels. I tuck a stray hair into my swimming cap with a shaking hand.

Hannah rotates her shoulders backward and then forward. She swims butterfly, which gives you really big shoulders, but she's not self-conscious about it; she just wears men's T-shirts. People love Hannah. She's fun. She has huge blond curly hair and big blue eyes and she never stops talking, organizing, and planning. She's been my best friend since we were six, and now, looking at how nervous she is, I find myself feeling protective even though I'm in the same position.

Well, not exactly the same; her parents are really pushy. She ignores it or it would drive her crazy. Mine think swimming is less important than either schoolwork or being a well-rounded human being—we agree to disagree.

Hannah's standing next to me now. She smiles and pulls at the front of my swimming cap. I fold my arms and pretend to ignore her. She pulls the elastic six inches away from my forehand and I brace for her to snap it, but instead she nudges her face next to mine and starts trying to pull my swimming cap over her head as well as mine. Ridiculous human being. This is why I bring spare caps.

I can't keep a straight face. I start giggling and help her pull the thick elastic further over her head. It hurts—her nose is digging hard into my cheekbone, but I'm determined to get it. *Beep!* Hannah's eyes widen at the sound of the whistle. This is her race!

She hurriedly pulls her head away, making her swimming cap ping off and nearly land in the pool. I can see a couple of officials looking very unimpressed at us. Sor-ree. Just trying to lighten a very heavy mood here. I dive to retrieve Hannah's cap while she fights her frizzy mop of hair into a bun.

We hug quickly and she hurries to the nearest pool, where the butterfly swimmers are waiting by the diving blocks. Some impressive shoulders in that group.

Now I'm alone and back to feeling sick and scared about my own race. I tuck my ears into my swimming cap, and everything becomes a smooth roaring noise.

An official comes to check my name against a list she has on her clipboard. I can't help but notice that she has a very fluffy top lip. She catches me staring at it and I quickly look down.

"Louise?" she asks.

"Brown," I say, to her shoe, and she ticks my name off.

She must be one of only ten people in the place who aren't feeling hysterical. If the fire alarm went off, I think we'd all run in circles, screaming and slapping our faces.

My race is called and I join a line of girls who look just like me. Tall girls with no hips, no boobs, and frizzy hair are the norm here. I'm going to fit in so well in the Training Camp! Finally, someone to borrow clothes from.

I look around for Debs, who coaches me and Hannah. She's standing by the pool where I'll be doing my race, arms folded, staring intently at me. She gives me a nod. She's not the most affectionate person. That nod means "Go on, Lou, I know you can do it! Supportive things, etc.!"

Up on the blocks I scuff my feet and stare dead ahead. You swim no one's race but your own.

The official nods and I bend into my dive, wrapping my fingertips over the edge of the block and swaying gently to loosen my hips. There's a pause that feels never-ending, and I focus on the spot in the water where I want my dive to take me.

The starting pistol bangs. There's an explosion of power from my legs, and I dive hard. I can hear the block rattle as I push away from it with all my strength. A cold, hard slap against my thighs, and I spring into butterfly stroke. Hannah's faster at this, but I'm pretty good too. I whip my arms up and over my head, my fingers then cutting into the water in front of my face. As my arms pull down, my hips tilt and my legs kick together like a mermaid tail. This is the closest I ever get to elegant.

Backstroke now, my second fastest stroke, and I hold my head steady as I stare up at the ceiling. I practiced this last night when everyone else had finished training. I count signposts on the ceiling so I don't ram my head into the side of the pool and slow myself down. Debs says this is the mind-set of a consummate pro.

I had to Google *consummate*. It's either a compliment or a French soup.

I feel so happy when I swim, strong and graceful and like everything is right with the world. This is my Thing.

The individual medley is a strange race—most people are slowest on the breaststroke, fastest on the crawl. I'm the other way around, so I always pull ahead on laps five and six, hopefully opening up enough of a lead that some freakish monkey-armed girl with a devastating crawl time can't catch me on seven and eight.

And here's seven and eight, harder in a pool where everyone's so powerful. The water is churned up and throwing me about. So much for feeling graceful—this is like fighting water. But I can't sense anyone on the left or right of me, so I must've pulled ahead. Excellent, it's all going according to plan.

Now it's about hanging on to this lead. I carve my right hand back past my face to make a groove in the water just long enough to turn my face and grab a huge, ragged breath. In this choppy water it's difficult, so each time I'm just praying I find air. I can't afford to choke.

Final lap and I'm completely in my rhythm. I know the end is approaching, but I have to keep swimming my hardest so no one catches me. I don't care if I smash my head into the edge of the pool—anything to maintain this speed to the end. My wrist hits something hard with a crack that I feel down to my hip, and I've done it.

I've done it! I won.

I fling my head out of the water, rip off my swimming cap and goggles, squeeze the water from my eyes, and look behind me. That's my first thought—how far behind are they?

But there's no one there.

They're all next to me. Everyone. There is *no one* behind me, no one still swimming.

The girl on my left looks bored; the one on the right is casually cleaning her goggles with spit. Oh my . . . *one of them is already out of the pool?!* I did that once, against a crap team in Swindon that was so slow I got out before the last girl finished. Debs yelled at me for that. Unsportspersonlike, she said.

Debs! Where is she, where's my coach? Maybe I swam extra lengths by mistake? That must be it. Hilarious, of course that's what happened. Dumb but understandable on a high-pressure day. This is *not* a Big Deal. Should I talk to someone, an official? Where is everyone going? Coach! Debs! Hello? No one is looking me in the eye. Did I *die* in that pool? Am I a ghost?

I might as well have. I came in last. For the first time since I started competing at ten years old, I was the slowest swimmer. I'm weak and cold. My legs are heavy as the adrenaline drops out of me. I don't know what to do . . . where to go. . . .

I have to find Hannah, and I look around frantically for her. There she is! She's throwing back her hair, laughing and shaking hands with an official who's handing her a slip of paper. She must have won her race. She catches my eye and her smile fades.

My best friend and I want to kill her.

chapter 1

my pillow smells. I should've changed the pillowcase weeks ago, but I haven't, and now it smells like my head. Which I did not realize was so smelly.

I can hear my family moving around downstairs, slamming drawers and clattering bowls. I'm not used to these morning noises because I'd usually be up at five a.m., grab my swim kit, and be training by six. Forty lengths of breaststroke, forty backstroke, forty crawl, ten butterfly, then a quick shower, sleepwalk through school, and be back in the pool by four p.m. YOLO!

But I haven't swum since the time trials three weeks ago, and now I'm stuck with a surprising number of useless hours. Who knew days were so long? I sometimes used to wonder what I was missing as I pounded out the lengths in the pool. Now I know. *No-thing.*

Except I'd never met our mailman before. He has a lot of nose hair. That's it.

My name's Lou and I am a fifteen-year-old ex-swimmer. I have an older sister, Laverne. Yup, Lou and Lav. We have a brother called Toilet.

That's a lie. It's just me, Lav, Mom, and Dad, in a small semi-detached house in the most boring town in the world.

So this summer I stopped swimming and I met our postman. And I finally got all that crying done that I've been meaning to do for ages, so that's good, isn't it? Plus I really explored the concept of Lying in Bed All Day Feeling Nothing but Despair. A summer lived right to the edges.

It's the first day of school. I'd mark the occasion by wearing a dress, but I don't own one. In our most private moments Hannah and I have accepted that the only way we'll find a dress to fit our shoulders is if we go to that cross-dressing shop in town. They've got nice stuff in the window; we'll cut the labels out.

It's also my first day without Hannah, as she's already left for the High Performance Training Camp in Dorset. She'll be there all term. Mom says that now that we're separated for a bit, I'll come out of Hannah's shadow. But she doesn't understand—I liked it there! I was very happy hanging out in it.

Going back to school would be fine if Hannah hadn't got through the time trials either. We could face it together, maybe hint that the competition was a big conspiracy. That we were *too* fast and we'd have threatened international relations at the next Olympics when we smashed everyone out of the water with our awesome times.

"Yeah, well, Russia," we'd have said, with careful looks around us. "They do *not* like silver, if you know what I'm saying." Then we'd have tugged our fedoras down and skulked off to double physics.

Wonder if the other side of my pillow is less smelly? I flip it. No.

But now Hannah has gone to the High Performance Training Camp without me and I won't see her all term. We're so far away from each other! She's in Dorset and I'm in Essex. She's heading to the Olympics; the most exciting place I'm heading is the bathroom.

Miraculously, it's free—pretty impressive in a house of four people, three of whom take showers you could time with a calendar.

I'm still using that special harsh shampoo for swimmers, the stuff that strips the chlorine out of your hair. Money is a bit tight at the moment, so Mom won't chuck it. I have to use it all up first, and we seem to have found a never-ending bottle. I soap my head and reflect that it really doesn't help that the smell reminds me of my old life.

I step out of the shower, fold a towel dress around me (the only kind I fit in, because it's sleeveless), and scuff my feet along the hallway. The carpet is worn in patches, so I'm careful not to catch my toe on a snagged thread. No one needs to start their day hopping and screaming.

I open my clothes drawer and drag out some jeans and a T-shirt—I don't have any "nice" clothes. Since I was eleven I've been caught up in some desperate, endless growth spurt. There's no point buying decent clothes, because they probably won't fit in a month's time. I'm five ten and *still* growing.

It's fine; if I ever get a boyfriend, I can carry him when he's tired.

I stab a wide-toothed comb gently into my hair because I don't have time to cut it out if it gets tangled. My hair doesn't grow down; it goes *out*, like Hannah's. We don't look like the princess in a fairy tale. We look like the enchanted vines that covered her castle for a hundred years.

It was always comforting to have a best friend who looked as different as I do. And we never minded, because we had swimming. We had a Thing. Now my Thing is gone and so has my friend.

I can't delay this much longer. I'm going to have to eat some breakfast and then . . . gah . . . *school*. I swing around the end of the banister and can't help smiling when I catch sight of my family.

The kitchen is too small for the four of us—we only fit in there if everyone stays very still. If you actually want to *move*, then elbows will get bumped and cereal will get tipped down backs. You know your house is cramped when you can start making a sandwich and end up in a food fight.

Dad is cooking (carefully), Mom's reading a book, and Laverne is troweling makeup onto her ridiculously beautiful face. They are such a good-looking family; they look like they're in an ad. They don't need a Thing. Everyone's just grateful they get to look at them.

I'm proud of them, but I wish I didn't look adopted.

Mom is half Indonesian, all curves and shiny brown hair and skin, while Dad looks like a doctor on a TV show. Good chin, nice teeth. Admittedly, he has a bit of a belly these days, but he just holds his breath for photos. Laverne is sixteen, with glossy black hair, actual boobs, and a tattoo that Mom and Dad don't know about.

Nature made her and then, a year later, took the same ingredients and made me. It's baffling. Good thing they didn't have a third child; it would probably have a face like a knee.

"Morning . . ." I sigh at the room, and they mumble back sleepy responses. Dad slides a brick of scrambled egg onto my plate as I sit down. Mom subtly slides Lav's makeup bag away from her.

"Enough, Laverne."

"A little more highlighter and blush and I'm *done*, I swear."

Mom keeps reading as she drops the makeup bag into a drawer next to her. Lav looks mutinous, but she's still got her mascara wand, so she makes good use of it before Mom reunites it with the bottle.

The mood in the kitchen is a little, well, moody. Lav's grounded because she was texting a boy late at night. I never have any boys to text, regardless of the time of day.

I poke up a forkful of egg and stare at it. Eyes down, I say, "Um. Caaaan I . . ."

"No," Mom says.

"You don't even know what I was going to say!"

Mom imitates my voice with annoying accuracy. "Can I not go to school today or maybe ever, can I just lie and get a job instead and we'll tell everyone at school that I changed my name, had plastic surgery, and made it onto Team Great Britain after all?"

Damn. Spot on.

Laverne finishes applying her thirty-second coat of mascara and leans toward me as if she's going to impart the secret of immortality.

Expectations low, I lean toward her.

"It's going to be OK at school," she says.

"Really?"

"Yes. Because no one cares about your swimming. Only you think it's a big deal."

"It *is* a big deal."

"Shut up, I'm trying to help you. I swear, if anyone even *mentions* swimming—which they won't—and you tell them what happened, they'll say, 'Huh.' And they won't ever think of it again. It's boring. No one cares. Amelia Bond from eleventh grade? She had her big hairy face mole removed over the summer. *That* is interesting."

I'm unconvinced but not willing to have an argument about it. Lav's wrong; it's not true that no one cares. Hannah cares. Hannah understands that swimming is extremely important. But thinking about Hannah feels like poking a blister, so I make myself stop.

Dad slings the frying pan into the sink. He does all the cooking. Mom's specialty dish is food poisoning.

"You girls ready to leave for school in ten?"

"Shotgun!"

"Lav! You always sit in the front!"

"Yes. Because I always call shotgun. Please stop me if this confuses you."

"Fine. Infinity shotgun!"

"You can't call infinity shotgun—everyone knows that," says Mom. "Now off you go."

"Are you home tonight, Mom?" I ask.

"Uh, no, I have a . . ."

"Daaa-ate," we all chorus.

"So go on, what's his name?" Lav asks.

Mom hesitates.

"It's OK," says Dad kindly. "If you don't know it, you don't have to pretend."

"You can check his wallet when he goes to the bathroom," Lav suggests.

"Though if he takes it with him, he's possibly not coming back," I finish.

Mom gives out three death stares and returns to her book.

Yeah, date. So it's a little odd in this house.

Mom and Dad divorced when I was little but are the nicest divorced couple. They never fight and they get along really well. I'm not sure why they divorced, but I don't want to ask in case the answer involves sex and I'll *never* stop being sick.

Dad lost his job last year and he had to move in with us until he finds a new one. It's taking a lot longer than he thought it would. Sometimes when he leaves his email open, I see all the rejections in his in-box.

It's not ideal. Lav and I have to share a room, but we don't say anything because we don't want to hurt his feelings. I worry about him. He gets up early every morning, like he's still got a job, and dresses in a suit and then just . . . I don't know . . . waits for the day to pass until we come home.

It's like having a professionally dressed but depressed dog.

Between me and him, this house hasn't been much fun this summer. No wonder Lav and Mom are dating like men are off to war.

We call goodbye to Mom and trudge out to the car. Lav forces me into the back, which is not easy. Three-door cars are such a lie; you can't call it three doors unless you see the trunk as an acceptable way to enter a car.

Laverne fiddles with the radio until she finds a pirate station. It sounds like people shouting in a cramped space. As if she doesn't get enough of that at home.

"Oh, Lav, you're so alternative. I cannot get my head around how nonmainstream you are." I sigh from behind my knees. "Move your seat forward."

Lav squeezes the lever and slowly pushes her seat back as far as it goes, crushing me into an even tighter S shape.

"It's garage, idiot."

"Is that the name of the music or just *where* they are? Come on, Lav, seat forward!"

"*Laverne!*" says Dad. "Move the seat forward or you can walk the rest of the way. Do you want to walk in those shoes? *Can* you walk in those shoes?"

I peer around to see what Dad's talking about. She's wearing black, studded, chunky boots—it looks like she's got weapons on her feet.

"Yes, I can! Not very far, or fast, or . . ."

"I don't know why you do that to your feet," Dad sighs.

"You don't get me, Mark," she sighs back dramatically.

"Dad!" he corrects her.

"No, Lav, *everyone* gets you," I say, defending him. "You're so instantly gettable that if you were an exam question, everyone would be happy to see you. And that's the only time they would be happy to see you, ha ha ha—ow! Legs legs legs!"

As Dad approaches the school gates, I can see a tall boy with long hair loitering. Lav slumps in the seat.

"Drive, drive, drive!" she hisses at Dad.

"What?" he asks, but drives past the school gates.

"Ah . . ." Lav sighs.

"Was that Beau Michaels waiting for you?" I say.

"Yes, and shut up. Dad, can you drop us at the back entrance, please?"

"Wait." Dad is puzzled. "Someone named their son *Beau* and that was allowed to happen?"

"Daaa-aad." Lav rolls her eyes.

"Like, no one was arrested? They were just allowed to do that to an innocent child?" he asks.

"You're not funny," Lav tells him firmly.

Dad circles a mini traffic circle and heads back to the school entrance.

"No, no, no!" Lav slumps down in her seat again. "I mean you're hilarious, Dad! Really, very witty!"

"I thought so," he agrees serenely, and we sail past the entrance again, poor Beau Michaels watching us with the dawning realization that all is not well in his love life.

Dad pulls up at the back entrance to school. Lav hops out and flips her seat forward, and I unfold myself into a normal shape. Well, normal for me.

"Come on, LouLou," says Dad.

I pick at some dry skin on my lip and look down. Maybe Dad will get bored of waiting and just let me sit quietly in the back of the car for a few years. Eventually I'll be old enough to shuffle forward and share the driving.

Lav leans down at my window.

"I *swear*," she says, "this isn't a big deal unless you make it a big deal. You *nearly* got to the Olympics. That's the closest anyone I know in this crappy little town has ever got to achieving anything! No offense, Dad."

"No, that's fine," he murmurs.

"So please, just don't even *mention* it. Now the school day begins, and you do not know me."

She wobbles away on her monstrous shoes. She looks like a baby gazelle. I can't imagine how dumb I look when I clump along behind her. Gazelle and the mammoth, off on their adventures.

That thought makes me even sadder, so I push it aside and give Dad a brave smile. My dry lip splits and bleeds.

"It's going to be a good day," he promises.

"OK," I mumble through blood and a semiclean tissue I found in the door handle. I clamber out of the car and follow Lav at the agreed-upon distance of six feet.

chapter 2

Weez!! I can't believe I've been here a week, time is flying!
People are nice, but I haven't scoped out any real friends
yet (you have no grounds for jel). I'm learning so much, I
thought everyone would be terrifyingly good, but I'm OK, you
know? Not saying I'm the best but I think I've got a chance.
I MISS YOU.

Hxxxxxx

av and I don't hang out at school—she's in the grade above, and
we're so different I'm not sure people know we're related. She's
pretty popular but seems to get in endless long-running fights with
other girls. She thinks they're intimidated by her maturity.

I think it's because she flirts with their boyfriends. We agree to
disagree.

I used to head into school with Hannah, exhausted and damp
from swimming, do some work, chat with some people (well, she

would; I'd hang out in her shadow—*happily*, thanks, Mom), then head back to the pool. Hannah and I always treated school like a chore, a little like the Queen snipping a ribbon on a hospital wing.

I don't think we missed much; our school is very ordinary. A horse walked onto the soccer field six years ago and people *still* talk about it.

But despite my whining, I have resolved to make an effort. Today I'm launching Operation: Make Friends. I'm an idiot for having only one friend. I needed a spare!

I'm so used to having Hannah's arm slung round me as she makes me laugh with nine years' worth of stupid private jokes. I've got all my halves of those jokes and nothing to do with them.

I feel shy as I enter my homeroom, so I check my bag to make me look busy, not lonely. Classic move. I delve through it, looking at my books and pencils. Yup, all there. Hi, guys.

I get so carried away with my acting that I trip, my backpack swings around with surprising force, and eight small objects fall out. What eight small objects, you ask?

Eight tampons.

ARGH!

What is *wrong* with tampons? Seems like every time I open my bag, they leap out in a group suicide bid. I haven't even started my period yet; they're just in case. My face burns with a blush as I crouch and start shoveling them back into my bag, desperate for this moment to end. It couldn't get worse.

Yes, it could. I feel a light tap on my head—someone is "helping" by throwing an escaped tampon at me.

And *then* Mr. Peters races in late. Perfect—the nicest teacher in school (and not bad-looking, actually, if you like cardigans) begins his morning by falling over me as I scrabble on the floor, chasing tampons and trying not to cry.

The class falls silent as he comes over and helps me to my feet. I like Mr. Peters; he's one of the few people in school taller than me, and not in a stooped, have-to-get-my-shoes-specially-made sort of way.

I give him a "thank you and that never happened" smile and weave through to our desk at the back. *My* desk, now. Teachers always knew they could sit Hannah and me there. We weren't particularly *good* students, but we were quiet. You don't need to pass notes to someone you've known that long.

I sit down, face still burning, and hope everyone develops amnesia by lunch. I don't want to be Tampon Brown all semester.

"Did you see that video I posted on your wall?" The two boys in front of me chat, and I lean forward to join in. After a bad start, Operation: Make Friends begins *right now*.

"Yeah! That guy looked so much like Hatsy it blew my mind."

"That's why I put it up there!"

"Oh, right! But everyone looks like Hatsy."

They collapse into quiet hysterics. For some reason.

I'm watching the conversation go back and forth, feeling the smile die on my face.

Who is Hatsy? Is it funny that everyone looks like him? Apparently. And what was that video? This conversation is like code; there's no way I can join in.

"Double history next, nightmare!" I say to the back of their heads in a friendly, eye-rolly sort of way. But too quietly, so they don't realize I'm talking to them. I look out the window and bite my nail. I'm not embarrassed, I'm busy! Busy biting this nail.

"Sorry, did you say something?" One of the boys turns around.

I nod, suddenly choking on a piece of nail. Now I'm coughing right in his face. *Right in his face.*

"No talking in the back!" Mr. Peters calls over. The boys turn back, one of them frowning and wiping his face.

I sit, stunned by my own social idiocy, and wonder if I will ever stop blushing or if my family can use my head as a radiator and cut their heating bills.

Then I'll have to be homeschooled, right?

My phone vibrates (it's up my sleeve) and I slide it out for a peek. It's a text from Mom, a picture of a badly stuffed otter. She may be grumpy in the mornings (and some afternoons and evenings), but she gets me—bad taxidermy always makes me laugh.

There's a picture of an annoyed-looking stuffed fox holding a handbag that never stops being funny, no matter how many times I look at it (and I needed to look at that fox a lot this summer). I scroll around my phone and then tap my in-box.

I really should reply to Hannah's last message. We've been chatting every day, but she starts all the conversations and I feel like everything I write is fake—things like *I'm sooooooo happy for yoooooo! Xxxxx.*

I'm a very bad liar.

After the time trials, I did my best to seem OK. I sat at the front of the minibus instead of at the back with Hannah, because I had suddenly developed "car sickness."

I kept staring up at the ceiling, because the fake car sickness was also making my eyes water. "Anyone else have wet eyes? I think it's the air-conditioning. Look, my eyes are so wet they're actually *leaking!*" (Sniff.)

Hannah had always been good, but I never realized she was

much better than me. I think she swam one of her fastest times ever that day. I don't know my time; officials don't chase after the girls who come in last.

Hannah was so excited and I didn't want to spoil it. That night I texted her loads, things like: *I'm so proud of you my fish!!! Xxxxxxx.* Which is a bit fake and gushy, but *You stole my dreams* is not a cool thing to text your best friend, even if it's true.

And I am happy for her! I'm just sad for me.

"Louise?" I look up. Mr. Peters is staring, and the kids in the class are starting to turn and roll their eyes. What have I done *now?*

"Yee-urp?" I say stupidly, and he smiles at me, a little exasperated, and says, "Sasha Burrows?"

Oh. The attendance. Right.

The morning begins with a double block of history, where I learn a lot of really cool things, like how *I know nothing about history* and *I am basically as educated as a piece of toast.*

See, *this* is the problem with planning to be a professional swimmer for the rest of your life; you don't think that you might need an education. Basically, the moment I could read, I felt educated enough. After that I used school time to relax in. Can't believe I hadn't noticed how behind I'd got. Clearly, Han and I were oblivious in our bubble of idiot.

My history teacher corners me after class to say, "How exciting about Hannah. You must be so proud!"

"Yes, yes, I am, I really am!" I say back at her, nodding hard with big, fake eyes.

History is followed by chemistry, because this school believes in putting the *boring* in *educa-boring-tion.*

It's amazing how little I know on this subject too. I listen hard and take lots of notes. Maybe I'm an academic genius; perhaps *that's* my actual Thing, not swimming after all.

"Any ideas? Anyone?"

I shoot my hand in the air.

"Louise!"

"Potassium!"

"No. Pota . . . what? I haven't mentioned potassium once this lesson."

"Oh, OK."

People snigger. The teacher stares at me, baffled. "Did you mean *phosphorus*?"

"Uh. Yeah?"

"That's still wrong."

Finally the morning's over and it's lunchtime. I follow the smell of cabbage until I'm at the cafeteria. (We hardly ever have cabbage; there's just this lingering smell. Mysterious.)

I look around. I knew this would happen. There's no one to sit with, and every table "belongs" to a friendship group, so I wouldn't just be eating there—I'd look like I was trying to join their group. I don't want to be ignored or, worse, told to get lost.

Can I bring my own little table into school every day?

I buy a sandwich, stick it in my backpack, and head outside, day-dreaming about my new (unlikely) future as a chemistry genius. My first breakthrough would be to disprove its credibility as a subject, forcing thousands of unemployed chemistry teachers to rethink their snotty attitudes.

I walk in a circle around school, eating my sandwich. It's boring to have no one to talk to. I take out my phone. I'm tempted to call

Hannah, but then we'll have to talk about training camp, and the thought of *that* makes my food stick in my throat.

As I'm choking and spluttering, eyes watering, phone in hand, Mr. Peters appears next to me. He raises his eyebrows at the phone, which I'm not allowed to have out during the school day. I wave it weakly and whisper, "Ambulance." He gives a snort of laughter and keeps walking.

He stops and turns back.

"Lou, you *are* joking?"

I nod, putting my phone away. He makes a "phew!" gesture and keeps walking.

Great, I've found someone I can chat to—and they're paid to talk to me.

As I'm putting my phone away in my bag, I realize I've stopped in front of the one place that can help me.

The library.

Home of the introverted and people too quiet to say, "No, Lou, I don't want to be your friend. Leave me alone to read. Get that friendship bracelet *off* me. No, *you* shush!"

chapter 3

I settle down in one of the booths and feel myself relaxing for the first time all day. I quietly finish the last of my sandwich, eyes darting around for the librarian. She's a small, nervy, hissing woman, and if that makes her sound like a terrifying animal, then *good*.

I'm in the sports section. It's only about a shelf long, but there's a tattered old book there called *Swimming for Women and the Infirm*. Brilliant! I pull it down and start reading. It smells musty and is adorably nuts, focusing on "making elegant, ladylike shapes" rather than actually going anywhere. I'd love to see the look on Debs's face if I tried this. "Personal best? No, I'm making a star shape, wheee!"

I haven't seen Debs in weeks. After the time trials she suggested I "take a break" from swimming, which was a pretty unsubtle dumping. My team had been training before school, after school, sometimes during lunchtime and on weekends, and we'd all been working toward these time trials. Now that I'd flunked, there didn't seem to be much point in carrying on training—I clearly wasn't good enough. I'd just get in everyone's way, being slow, crying, trailing ribbons of snot behind me. . . . I thought of asking for another chance. I could always try out next year, but what if I came in last *again*?

I told Hannah this on our last sleepover of the summer. It was still warm out, so we were camping—our last chance before she'd be off to Dorset. As I babbled on about my worries, she looked uncomfortable. Of course, she's my best friend; she wasn't going to say, "Yeah, train for another year! I'm sure you won't choke *this* time!" But she also couldn't say, "Give up, pal, you're clearly awful."

We sat, chewing in silence. I was eating cereal out of the box. Hannah was eating concentrated Jell-O, which is disgusting, but she thinks it stops her nails from splitting from all the chlorine in the pool. Plus side, she always smells fruity.

Thankfully for her, she was saved from giving me career advice. "SLUG!"

There was a huge one shuffling its disgusting belly up the inside of our tent. Our screams brought Hannah's mom out to the yard. (Because, yes, of course we were camping in the backyard—we're not heroes.)

Barbra'd just got in from a shift at the hospital and she wasn't in the best of moods. When you work in the ER, two girls crying over a slug can seem dumb. She flicked it mercilessly into the hedge, ignoring our pleas to (a) be gentle and (b) escort it to a leaf ten or twenty miles away, please.

Babs (as I have *never* dared call her) then popped her head back into the tent and stared at me for a moment with a concerned look on her face.

"Lou, have you *done something* to your hair?"

She looked horrified. Classic Babs. She's got all the tact of a brick, as Mom said when she thought I wasn't listening.

"No," I said honestly, trying to flatten it.

"*Bye, Mom!*" said Hannah pointedly. Babs made a face like "What have I done *now*?" and went back to the house.

It's not a competition, but I definitely win the moms.

After a quick debate about the chances of that slug sliming to the top of the tent and falling into one of our sleeping mouths—which we had to stop because Hannah was laughing and dry-retching so hard I thought she might choke—we returned to the all-important subject of *me*.

I told her I was going to stop swim training and how it was actually exciting because maybe I'd find something that I'd be really good at, something cooler than swimming, I said pettily, and immediately felt bad as she started trying to help.

"International supermodel?"

Yes, well, obviously, I said. That's plan B. But I'm scared of flying.

Hannah chewed thoughtfully on a cube of Jell-O. "The thing is," she says, "you've been swimming since you were like eight . . . ?"

"Seven," I corrected her.

"Right. So there're so many options you haven't explored! Loads of things you could be amazing at!" She was so excited by how brilliant I'd be. It made me feel tired and irritable and not very brilliant.

Suddenly a shadow loomed against the side of the tent, and Hannah's dad, Damian, called our names. He unzipped the front flap.

"Are you girls smoking?" He looked at us narrowly.

"No!"

"Make sure you don't. It's a filthy habit." He zipped us back up and left me and Hannah rolling our eyes at each other. Her parents are so weird. You can't just randomly bark at your daughter, "Don't do drugs! Don't smoke! Don't get pregnant!" and call it parenting.

I laugh out loud now, remembering how last month Dad thought Laverne was pregnant because she was so tearful and shifty. He very sweetly said we could cope with anything as a family.

Lav cried, hugged him, and confessed she'd left her eye shadow in her jacket when she put it in the wash and now all his clothes were glittery.

I suddenly remember I'm in the library, laughing like a loon by myself. The librarian narrows her eyes, and a gang of girls stare at me like I'm insane. I duck my face behind *Swimming for Women and the Infirm* and pretend I'm engrossed. *Oh look, she's floating* and *pointing a toe. What an athlete.*

The rest of the day is OK; it doesn't get better, but it doesn't get worse. I had been dreading going back to school, thinking everyone would be all, *Oh my god, you came last in the time trials?! But Hannah got through? That's so embarrassing for you, are you OK, are you going to cry? What are you going to do now? What's that coming out of your eye, are you* crying??

But, I hate to say it, Lav was right. No one cares. I don't think anyone even notices. And if that makes my first day back at school sound a little boring, then BINGO! That's because it is.

I see Laverne heading toward the parking lot at the end of school with a gaggle of friends. I want a gaggle. I join her and give her friends a little wave as they leave, which they're too cool to return.

They're the sort of people who always make me feel sweaty and worry that I smell like food or I've got something between my teeth.

"How was the first day?" Lav asks.

I give a bland little "meh." That sums it up.

"I was right, wasn't I?"

I have to admit it. "Yeah, no one really cares. It's not a big deal."

"No, about Amelia Bond's hairy face mole. She looks normal, but you know something's missing."

"Like there's a ghost on her face?"

"*Yes!*"

chapter 4

the next few days get a little less "meh"—I make an effort to chat with people in my classes, and they're not unfriendly. It's just everyone already has friends and they're not looking for new recruits, so I spend my lunchtimes hanging out in a largely empty library. I even read the occasional book— seems rude not to—but it's not the same as having a real-life friend.

By Thursday I'm thoroughly bored of eating a sandwich hidden in a book, and all morning I've been thinking about going to see Debs, my coach. Ex-coach.

Six and a half weeks is the longest I've gone in years without seeing her, but I felt shy after the time trials. She says things like "Silver is just first place loser!" so I wasn't sure how she'd treat an *actual* loser.

Plus I didn't have swim training, and I didn't feel I could just turn up on her doorstep: "Hiyaaaa. Let's ignore the twenty-five year age gap and hang out! You can blow your whistle at me and I'll wear wart remover strips if that makes it less weird."

There's a public pool next to my school; the school swim team trains there. I've been stumping my way up this path every morning for years, with a heavy sports bag over my shoulder and sleep crust scratching at my eyes. Today I buy my sandwich and head there instead of to the library, rubbing my eyes out of habit.

It seems empty, but I can hear some noise in the distance, girls chatting. I wonder if it's the girls I used to train with. We weren't best friends, but after a lonely week, I'd be really happy to see them now. As long as Cammie isn't there—she's rude, rich, and mean. She intimidated me and Hannah and we hated that she did.

I follow the sounds and it takes me to the changing room. I push my way through the heavy door and get a big whiff of chlorine and shampoo.

The door shuts loudly behind me and fifteen half-dressed girls with wet hair go quiet and stare at me. The silence hangs, heavy and awkward and smelling of feet.

Not such an exciting smell anymore. Oh, and there's Cammie. Great. One foot up on the bench, moisturizing her legs, she's halfway through a story and looks up to see who's dared to interrupt her.

A couple of girls give me small smiles, but they look a little embarrassed. It's weird when semi-naked people are embarrassed for *you*.

I suddenly feel I'm not meant to be there; this isn't the welcome I'd expected. Everyone goes back to getting dressed. Cammie picks up where she left off, loudly. Following her lead, everyone ignores me.

"All right, Lou?" says a tall, muscular girl who's drying in between her toes. She says it quietly, like she doesn't want everyone to hear.

One person cares! (But I can't remember her name. Aargh!)

"Yeah, I'm good, thanks." Mellie? Probably not. Who would call a kid Mellie? It rhymes with Smelly

"I . . . uh . . . just came to say hi. So . . . hi."

"Hi," says Smelly. (Mella? Maybe.)

"And also I forgot my . . . this. Yes, this." I'm babbling to fill the awkward silence as I open my old swimming locker and find a dusty nose clip. "Excellent," I say, and pop it in my pocket.

Cammie frowns and says, "Why do *you* need *that*?"

There's a shocked silence and a couple of embarrassed giggles, swiftly muffled. (It would've been more polite to *not laugh*, but whatever.) My heart starts beating harder and I can feel my ears going red with anger, but I don't let it show.

"Just to block out that smell, Cammie. You reek of eggy hair-removal cream."

Zing!

Shame I only thought of it before I fell asleep that night.

My actual "sassy retort" was to give a weak smile and leave, closing the door gently behind me. Oooh, *burn*.

This place is my *home*, or it used to be. But clearly my pathetic performance at the time trials makes me an embarrassment to the team. Wish Lav could've seen that, her and her "no one cares, it's not a big deal."

I see how shallow they are. I'm full of rage about how the world isn't Winners or Losers, we're all just people, guys, special snowflakes with a lot to offer the world!

To enjoy this self-righteousness, I have to forget that I was *exactly* like this until a month or two ago. La la la la la la, let's just ignore that uncomfy fact.

I head for the pool to find Debs. After Hannah, she's the closest thing I've got to a friend. As I enter the pool area, I can hear the splashing of the next swim class. These guys are younger, but they're still good. I watch them dart through the pool with swift movements and slightly shaky tumble turns.

Debs is striding up and down in tiny shorts (all year round, tiny shorts—maniac!) shouting at anyone who stops. You can't stop during training. Your muscles cool down and you're less effective; you've got to just power through the pain. Debs always said that was one of my great strengths.

She spots me and I wave.

She shouts something that I can't hear over the thunderous noise from the pool.

"What?" I smile and point at my ears.

"No outdoor shoes."

Um. Right.

"I'll go, then. I just came to say hi!"

She gives me a brief smile and goes back to watching the swimmers. She was never one for the soft and cuddlies, but I was expecting at least a hug, perhaps a circling back pat at the end? (I would *like* a hug with a circling back pat at the end, dammit! I deserve one. I've had a very hard summer and she should understand.)

She doesn't look up again, but that's cool—she's busy, and I don't want to be paranoid. So I sit on a bench at the back of the viewing platform and eat my sandwich (quickly, as the humidity makes it soggy. Bit gross.)

I try to add up how many hours I've spent at this pool: an hour a day before and after school five days a week, plus the odd lunch hour, then two hours on Saturday morning pretty much every week since I was seven. My mind boggles and I get out my phone to use the calculator.

I think, (a) no wonder my hair is so crispy—that's a lot of chlorine, and (b) I can't do math either! What I don't know would fill a barn, as my old gran would say.

I've never sat in the viewing area before. I watch the swimmers and feel drowsy at the repetitive splashing, broken up with occasional short, sharp pips from Debs's whistle. After all these years I know exactly what each sound means. "Go faster, you're slowing down, I'm watching you, keep your arms crisp, don't drag those legs! ALWAYS SWIM FASTER!"

Debs doesn't have a sound for "You're doing really well, guys, and remember it's just a sport, let's have some fun!" I snicker to myself at the thought of what that would be—a snotty squeak as she choked on her whistle.

My head droops in the warmth. It's dull watching people swim, and I think about the hours my poor family has spent up here on these uncomfortable benches, slapping supportive looks on their faces like they could *not* think of anywhere else they'd rather be on a Saturday morning. "What, the *park*? On this sunny day?! You must be kidding. Let's go sit somewhere noisy and damp. I'm happy to hug the dishwasher or we can watch you swim *again*."

Dad and Lav can both sleep sitting up. They probably learned how to do it here.

My phone vibrates. I *bet* it's Hannah. I go to tell her about the girls in the changing room. Then I realize that if *she* walked in there, everyone would be excited to see her.

I stare at the water until my eyes go blurry and I force myself to not blink, when I have that unmistakable feeling that someone's looking at me. I must look demented, like I'm in a staring competition with the water.

I glance over my shoulder. There's a field outside the swimming pool, and right now there's a boy on it. He's a few feet from the window but close enough that I can see he's good-looking, small and sort of cool-without-trying. His skin is so clear he looks like a model. I finger my chapped lips.

He's kicking a ball against the wall, which I could do—however, he's looking up at me while he's doing it, and I'd lose a tooth to a misaimed kick if I tried that. I stare at him gormlessly.

Just then a bigger version of him walks past the door. Aaah, I knew he looked familiar; he must be related to Roman Garwood. Roman is two years older than me. He is *basically* physical perfection, and if I had more of a grasp on sex (so to speak), I'm sure I'd be feeling all sorts of inappropriate things for him.

I don't know Roman; he's never spoken to me. But I've overheard him talking to older girls and he's pretty rude—blunt and prickly. (*Why* does that make him more attractive?

Roman takes his sweater off to reveal broad shoulders and muscled arms. The shorter boy catches me staring at aforementioned muscles and smiles at me. Even by today's low standards this is embarrassing. I give him a small, no-teeth smile back. This smile says, "Yup, I was staring at your brother like a dog at a sausage. Let's never mention this ever again."

A third boy joins them, pulling off his sweater too, which makes his T-shirt ride up over a muscled chest. I examine my cuticles. It's hard to know where to look around here.

The *new* guy, also quite ridiculously handsome, is fidgety; he pulls his T-shirt down, then takes the ball from Small Roman and starts doing keepy-uppies. The three of them seem dejected and look like they're arguing in a halfhearted way.

Actually, I recognize that third boy! He's not at our school anymore; he must be three years older than me. But a couple of years ago, when he was still an upperclassman, I had won some big county competition. I'd been messing around in the car with Mom, wearing my medal and pretending her Ford Focus was doing a victory parade for me. I'd forgotten to take the medal off when she dropped me at school, so I sneaked in late to assembly still wearing it. This guy had seen me and said something that had made everyone around him stare at me and then laugh 'til they couldn't breathe.

I'll never know what he said, and he probably wouldn't even remember, but it ruined something important to me.

Pete. That's his name.

Remembering that is the last straw for me today, and I shoulder my backpack and head back to school, I doubt Debs even looks around. I keep my head down and don't talk to anyone, don't answer any teachers' questions, for the rest of the day. Operation: Make Friends is on hold, possibly forever.

I *suspect* this school is tragically and unluckily full of dickheads and is no place for me to find a friend. Maybe I'll just sit tight and hope Hannah flunks out of training camp!

I don't mean that.

I think I do.

She could just get a muscle injury. Not disabling, but permanent, so she'd have to give up on her dreams and I'd have someone to talk to at lunchtime. (No, *you're* selfish.)

That night Dad makes us savory pancakes because Mom is out

on another date. I lie about how well school is going (I'm sure Lav knows the truth, but she says nothing) and head upstairs after watching a movie with Dad.

I lie in bed listening to Lav texting and WhatsApping (so many pings!) and settle down to sleep. I can hear Mom come in. She must've had a few drinks, because she's loud, clattering around getting her shoes off.

I know, without even checking, that Dad was waiting up for her. She heads straight to the kitchen, immediately in full flow, ranting about her evening. Not a great date, I guess. I hear Dad laugh, the fridge clunks, and then there's a *tiss tiss* as two beers are opened.

I hear my parents chatting and laughing as I drift off. It's nice. I'm glad they're still friends. I remember when we were younger and they'd have polite conversations over our heads, Mom gripping my shoulders so tightly it hurt. I remember . . .

Suddenly: "Just to block out that smell, Cammie. You reek of eggy hair-removal cream" pops into my head.

And a minute later:

Melia! That girl's name is Melia.

Thanks, brain.

chapter 5

the next day I wake up feeling less pathetic. I'm going to have a talk with Debs. I was her favorite swimmer—I will *make* her care about me again! I'm going to catch her when she's not busy, first thing in the morning, before classes start. When I head downstairs, there are four empty beer bottles in the kitchen. Mom and Dad will be grumpy this morning. Glad I'm missing that.

I leave Dad a note saying I'm walking to school and head off, feeling adventurous in the chilly, damp morning.

I go straight to Debs's office, which is unlocked and has coffee cooling on her desk. Excellent, she should be back soon. I sit in a chair (although not the one behind her desk—I wouldn't dare). She takes ages. I'm stuck eyeing her bookcase full of trophies for fifteen boring minutes. Eventually she walks in.

"There you are!" I shout.

"ARGH!" she shouts back. OK, that was a little bit of an ambush.

She holds her heart and looks irritably at me as she heads to her seat and flips open her laptop.

She doesn't seem delighted to see me, which is pretty flat lemonade from a woman who threw me in the air when I won gold at the County Championships last year. No one has attempted to throw me anywhere since I was in diapers, and even then there were probably anxious people yelling, "Lift with your legs, not your back!"

"Nice summer, Lou?"

NICE SUMMER?! How very dare she.

"Not great, Debs."

"Have you spoken to Hannah?"

Woohoo, someone else who wants to talk about Hannah.

"Yeah, she seems fine. Now, *I* . . ."

"I hear she's shaved a second off her personal best in individual already. I've said if she stays focused, she can almost certainly take another one off, although of course it won't be as quick as the first improvement. It never is."

She looks at me intently as she talks about Hannah. *Now* I have her full attention. I feel small. I look down at my hands and pick at a cuticle.

"Aaaaanyway, Debs." (Back to me, please.) "It's weird not training every night. I don't really know what to do with myself."

I'm hoping she'll understand and say something helpful. I look up from my hands and all I get is a view of the top of her head. She's checking her email.

"Yeah, my last bunch of burnouts said the same. I think they all got boyfriends!" She laughs as if she's said something funny. I must've missed that part.

"I'm a burnout?" I say, noticing how wobbly my voice has gone. She finally looks up.

"Lou, are you *upset* with me?"

"No," I lie. "Are you disappointed in me?"

"No," she lies. "But your turns weren't tight enough and your backstroke was nowhere up to your usual standard. Your arms just weren't strong enough on the day. So you got the result you got. You burned out, it happens."

I stare at her. "OK, Debs, only winners welcome in here. I get it." I stand up to leave, really slowly, giving her time to yell, "Lou! I didn't mean it to sound like that! Of course I don't care if you win or lose; we're pals. I was just being tough love with you because I care and I want to help you get over this."

I bend down and tie my shoelaces in silence, then retie them because emotional outbursts can't be rushed. Especially from a woman with the tenderness of a rock. I finally look up and realize that she's not teetering on the edge of anything emotional—she's just checking her email again.

Well, this first week at school has sucked, but it has taught me many things:

1. I have no friends.
2. This probably won't change, as no one in my class likes me, except as a tampon dartboard.
3. I am basically uneducated.
4. I'm *really* good at pretending I'm not about to cry.

I put number four into practice as I leave Debs's office. I don't want to enter my homeroom with a wobbling chin and blotchy eyes—"Damn this early autumn hay fever, right?" I don't want to go home and worry Mom, and I don't want to cry in public. That just leaves the one place that still makes me feel safe.

39

I scoot along the corridor to the pool, head down, hoping no adult will stop me and question my loose interpretation of the school rules. I'm glad to hear nothing from the locker rooms and there's no one in the pool, so I'm left in peace to sit on one of the poolside benches and watch the steam floating over the top of the water.

I start to cry, and it very quickly turns into one of those enjoyable sessions. When it's a relief to let it all out and you feel so much better. I think of every sad thing that's ever happened to me and wallow in self-pity.

Once I reach our dog, Mr. Hughes, who died peacefully of fat old age five years ago, it's clear I've run out of things to cry about.

After a while I subside into hiccups and dry my eyes. I root around in my bag for a tissue and find an old bathing suit, zipped up in an internal pocket and forgotten. Oh well, I think, it's not like I'll be using this again. So I blow my nose in it.

I feel much better, though I can tell that my face has already gone puffy. I'm such an ugly crier. I look like boiled ham glazed in snot.

I hear a noise across the pool and I freeze, holding the bathing suit/hankie to my streaming nose. Pete is lounging in the open doorway of the swimming pool. I think he's flicking away a cigarette.

I don't want him to see me covered in snot. (Admittedly, who *would* you want to parade your snotty face in front of?)

Cammie appears out of the changing room; she must've had extra training. She gives him an approving look.

"Waiting for me?" she asks, flirty and confident.

"Nope," he says. She smiles; he's obviously joking.

But he looks around as if the person he wants to see isn't there, and heads off down the sloping field to the parking lot.

Cammie looks outraged. She obviously can't believe he was that rude to her. I wonder how much angrier she'd be if she knew I'd seen that. I sit very still. *Please don't look back.*

My phone vibrates with a text, and her head whips around to me. She looks embarrassed but quickly recovers. If she were a cat, she'd be popping her claws out.

"Oh my god, are you sitting here *crying* over the swimming pool?" she asks with an incredulous smile. I grab my bag and scramble for the door Pete left through.

It's undignified to run away from Cammie, but I can't bear the thought of being laughed at. I stumble through the door and run down the muddy slope, picking up speed as I approach the parking lot.

I'm running so fast now that I couldn't stop if I wanted to, which is a real shame, because suddenly a car swings toward me as it pulls out of the lot. I try to jump out of the way but fall onto the hood of the car, sliding all the way across it and landing on my feet on the other side.

I'm OK! I half laugh, half gasp in shock, and look back at the driver. It's Pete. His mouth is hanging open, there's a muddy smear across his hood thanks to Yours Truly's butt, and I think he's going to yell at me. I do the only thing I can think of: I run away.

chapter 6

Weeeez, did you get my last email? Have you fallen down a
well or have you forgotten about me? I miss you so much. I'm
sorry, I don't know what to say. I wish we'd both got in. It's
cool here, but there's no one like you. They talk about swimming ALL THE TIME. If *I'm* saying that, think how bad they must
be. I'm like—let's just look at a fox in some wellies and chillax
guys?! Email me back!

Hxxxxx

I'm being unfair to Hannah. We usually email or text every single
day. But I hate hearing about the High Performance Training
Camp. I know I'm selfish, but whenever she messages, I feel a jealous, sicky surge in my stomach.

I want to be a better friend than that, so on Saturday morning I
write a long email back. I don't tell her how crappy I'm feeling. I
don't want her to feel guilty that she's not here, so I keep it all a bit
vague and bland.

The weekend passes *so* quickly. How does time move so slowly at school and then whiz past on Saturday and Sunday? I wish I had friends to hang out with. I try not to think about what everyone else is up to or it'll make me feel too sad.

I help Dad in the yard, and Mom offers to take me shopping, but I don't want to bump into girls from school out with my mom. I'd feel like a social reject. Lav's stuck at home too, since she's grounded, so she's reading in her room for most of the weekend and slathering some foul-smelling muck into her hair to "bring out the shine."

Out from where?

Dad makes her sit in the backyard so she doesn't stink up the house, and she sulks on the patio for about an hour while it "sinks into her follicles." She and Dad get snappy with each other, and then she says if she had a *decent* allowance, she could just go to the salon, like her friends do.

Ouch. Dad's sensitive about money. I try to give Lav a "shut uuup" look underneath her crusty hair muck, but it's too late. Dad disappears into the shed, and the sounds of talk radio come wafting out.

All too soon I get that Sunday-night feeling, and Lav and I are watching a wildlife documentary in the living room, in which loads of little worms are darting in and out of holes on the seabed.

"Beau Michaels," Lav says to me unexpectedly.

I frown at her, mystified, until she pokes her tongue out in tentative, jerky little movements.

Ew! I hit her with a pillow. Lav makes kissing sound like a fight between teeth and spit where no one wins.

Mom is watching us with narrowed eyes, so we go back to watching the Beau Michaels worms, stifling our smirks. I wish I were an adult and I could just stay in the house, where I feel safe, instead of having to drag myself to school five days a week.

I'm brooding on this five-out-of-seven ratio when there's a crashing noise from the kitchen. Lav and I jump. The back door has swollen in the heat, so the only way to come through it is dramatically loud and fast. If we had a cat, it would have a flat nose by now.

Dad marches into the living room, brushing cobwebs off his shoulders. I didn't realize how long he'd been out there. He smells like Uncle Vinnie, which is a polite way of saying *drunk*.

It's not polite to Uncle Vinnie, obvs.

"Have you been in the shed all this time?" Lav asks.

"Yes," he says.

"Doing what?"

"Working."

She opens her mouth to say "On what?" but he leaps in before she can.

"Well, everything in the house is bloody broken, isn't it? I'm run bloody ragged trying to fix everything because you all live in squalor!" The three of us look around the spotless living room, then at each other. We have no idea what he's talking about.

"Uh, I'm sorry?" says Mom cautiously. "I just find, you know, what with breeding fight dogs in the kitchen and all my drug dealing at the strip joint, housework does get past me."

I try not to laugh. I know Dad's going through a tough time, but yelling at us won't help. And I *did* give him my bedroom so he could have his own space and I could live squashed between

Lav's millions of bras and shoes, so, you know, a thank-you might be nice?

"The lamp in the kitchen was broken!" he says accusingly. "I had to take it apart."

"Oh, is it fixed? Thanks," says Lav, to make peace.

There's a pause. "No," Dad says eventually. "It's in bits now, isn't it? Now I have to put it together again, haven't I?"

He seems to be waiting for something.

"Thank you?" I offer.

He stomps back to the shed.

"Hide your valuables," Mom advises. "When Granny went into a home, he dismantled the TV and we never got it back together. It's how he copes."

I scroll around on my phone. Nothing back from Hannah. Good—I don't want to hear any more exciting tales of Training Camp tonight, especially now that the mood in the house has gone so sour.

I feel so tired. I kiss Mom and head up to bed. Through the landing window I can see Dad's shed, a patch of light in the darkness of the yard, where now the bushes have become pitch-black, evil-looking shapes.

In the middle of the evil I can see Dad's silhouette as he sits in his shed, bent intently over whatever he's working on.

Probably peeling apart a blender. It hurts my heart to watch him. He looks vulnerable, and for the first time I realize that he's getting old.

I send Han a message.

X.

45

She replies immediately.

X in your face.

I do have a friend who cares about me. She's just, you know, living our dreams while I rot in a double block of physics.

chapter 7

the next morning I wake up to the sound of Lav stretching and making agonized noises. She's so bad at mornings. I have had to put up with this drama every morning since I quit swimming. I wish Mom would just let her have espresso.

Like she's got anything to complain about! *I* have to have another crappy friendless day, then another, then three more, and then it'll be the weekend and hopefully I can fake my own death or run away or suddenly become eighteen and get a job? PLAN.

Suddenly I hear a screech from downstairs. Lav and I exchange alarmed looks, then swing our legs out of bed and race from our bedroom, pushing to get through the door first. Lav realizes her pajamas are a bit skimpy and doubles back to make herself decent.

Mom is bent over the kitchen counter sifting through a pile of soggy junk mail, peeling something off the back of a takeout pizza menu. I hope *both* my parents haven't gone crazy. Who'll raise me? I still need so much parenting.

"Are *you* making that noise?" I ask.

"Yes!" she cries without looking up. "Quickly, get some black clothes on."

"Black clothes?" says Lav, who's inserted herself into her skinny jeans and is now behind me. "Are we going to commit burglary?"

"Emergency mime?" I suggest. (Pretty pleased with that.)

"No!" Mom wails. "Your uncle . . ." She peers closely at the peeled-off piece of wet mail. ". . . Hamish, no, *Harold*, died last week. Your auntie just called. The funeral is today—it's in an hour. Quickly, get dressed!"

That's *so* much information in one sentence. Lav and I are staring at each other, having a long sleepy think when Dad enters the kitchen dressed as if he's off to work.

I hate this, but Mom says we have to let him if it makes him feel better.

"Who's dead?" he asks.

"Harold," says Mom. "Or Hagrid?" She squints at the blotchy ink on the funeral card. Mom has a very big family, and new uncles and cousins-twice-removed regularly crop up out of nowhere. It's impossible to keep track.

"I don't know a Hagrid," Dad muses.

"I think you missed your chance," I point out, which makes him smile and me feel good.

"*Excuse me!*" snaps Mom, looking up from her paper mush. "Is anyone listening? We have eight minutes to get out of the house and to this funeral, and I'm not taking you girls in your pajamas. Go, go, go!" She chases us upstairs.

I rush to the bathroom before Lav can get in there—she has never had a quick shower in her life. As I soap up, I realize that this

48

means a day off school! Thank you, Uncle Hester. We may never have met, but you have done your loving niece a favor.

Seven minutes later we're all dressed up, in the car, and heading for a church that Dad can't find on his phone. Lav and I are trying to dry our hair with the car heater. It's not working out well, but Mom keeps shoving our heads down in front of the vents, insisting we need five more minutes until we're funeral-appropriate. My sore neck does not appreciate this, but any minute not spent in school is fine by me.

Dad is staring at his phone, sweeping it around in big movements. He hits me on the head, but I have bigger problems, leaning between the front seats to get Lav's secondhand heater air.

The second time, however, he whacks me on my cold ear and it really hurts.

"Oi!" I protest. "Don't hit your kids."

"Sorry!" he sighs. "The phone just doesn't know where we are."

"Are the gravestones a hint?" asks Mom acidly, and we both look up to find we're driving past a graveyard and toward a church. Dad looks sheepish and pockets his phone.

We have to run around the church one and a half times before we actually locate the door. We're not church people, so we have no idea what to do with one. It's like when I see new swimmers come to my pool and stare at the footbath in confusion. "Is this the pool for nervous swimmers?"

We find a massive oak door that looks like our best bet. Dad pushes to open it, but nothing moves; he just looks like he's leaning against it, posing for a catalog. After watching him lean for a while, going redder and redder, we realize he needs help. The door opens slowly, with a haunted-castle-style creak, and we get it open about a foot. Mom and Lav slip through the gap first.

Dad pats his paunch and waves me through next. On the other side I bump into Mom and Lav, who have frozen in horror because they've emerged at the front of the church, next to the priest.

They stand and smile at him like fans.

He ignores us, which is kind of weird. Does this happen to him a lot? He must be really good at priesting.

We're looking out at a full church—there are like a hundred people here! Uncle Hebrides was *popular*. I give the room a weak smile and Dad saves the day. Taking Mom and Lav by the arm, he leads his moron family down the aisle, flashing a big charming smile left and right at stony-faced family members while I follow, trying to look like their caregiver.

Dad spots an empty pew near the back and pushes the three of us toward it. A woman in the row behind shakes her head at us, but I can't work out if it means "You people are terrible" or "How sad Humphrey is dead" or what. We all slide along the hard wooden bench as the priest continues his sermon.

Then we realize what that headshake meant: "Don't sit there—the bench is broken!" She really could've made her message clearer. But she didn't, so now the four of us are basically sitting on a seesaw. Dad shifts slightly, and Mom at the other end of the row wobbles as her side shoots up a foot. We all freeze and do Big Eyes at each other.

I had automatically propped my feet up on the seat in front, standard practice for a tall person facing teeny legroom, so I take them off and try to plant them on the floor for balance. This makes the bench lurch even more dramatically, and we all grab each other in panic.

Now Dad's end of the bench starts sinking; whatever the pew was resting on seems to be buckling at his end. Lav slides down toward him with the little hiss of butt on wood. Despite my best efforts, I begin to follow her. Mom is hanging on to the other end of the pew so she goes nowhere.

Dad is maintaining an admirably straight face as his bottom sinks lower and his knees move closer to his chin, and he manages to keep his eyes on the priest, nodding occasionally like, "Hmm good point, what *is* community?"

Thankfully, we're so late we've missed half the service, so we only have to sit like this for about twenty minutes. As the service comes to an end, the priest tells everyone to kneel and pray, but that is not an option in the Pew of Askew, so we all just duck our heads very slowly, trying to look respectful.

If I shift my butt, I'll flick Mom at the priest.

People are beginning to stare. I'm staring back, and I can't see anyone I recognize. Mom's family is so big. The moment the funeral is over, the mourners head for the doors, and we wait for the last person to leave before we attempt to move.

"OK," says Dad. "One . . . two . . . three . . . and up!" We all stand together. Success!

Almost.

Lav loses her footing, staggers, and falls, dragging me down with her, and I can't say Mom makes the smoothest dismount either. Dad helps us all up, shaking his head.

"Right," says Mom demurely, tucking her blouse in. "I think we should skip the buffet."

Dad agrees and we skulk out a side door and into the car. I'm still shutting my door as Mom puts the car into reverse. She's like a getaway driver.

We drive home to KISS FM—Lav called radio shotgun. I don't think that's a Thing, but Mom said not to squabble on holy ground, so I let I slide.

"Who was it?" I ask Lav as she flicks through the service pamphlet she picked up on the way out.

"Hmm?"

"Who was the funeral *for*?" I ask, jiggling the pamphlet so she can't read it until she pays me some attention. "Hugo? Heathcliff? Hubert?"

She tuts and flicks to the front page.

"Violet," she snaps, and pulls it back to read. She looks up a moment later and frowns. "Violet?"

Dad gives a snort of laughter, but I don't understand. Lav slaps her hand over her mouth, her big brown eyes horrified. Is this a sex thing?

It's usually about sex when everyone gets it except me.

I don't see how, though. "Dad?"

Dad twists in his seat to look back at me and say, "Wrong church, wrong funeral."

We gate-crashed a funeral?

We sit in stunned silence.

"That's awful," I breathe.

"Don't!" cries Mom. "I feel terrible."

"So you should!" Dad says. "No one in that church was related to you, and you didn't even notice!" (Mom is laughing.) "I'm glad there are only four of us, or you'd be getting us muddled with the pizza delivery boy!"

As I continue drying my hair in the heat from the vent, I realize I haven't thought about swimming in about an hour and a half. Which is a new record for me. I feel encouraged. Maybe I am going to cheer up and get normal.

A month ago I wouldn't have believed this was possible. It's like when I had the norovirus and I puked for hours until I felt like a deflated balloon. I couldn't imagine ever leaving the bathroom.

However, there's still a long list of Things That Are Rubbish About Lou Brown's Life. And the latest item is, I'm not about to get a day off school, because Mom craftily stowed our schoolbags in the trunk this morning.

She pulls up at the school gates and looks back at me.

"How is it, honestly?" she asks. Lav is fixing her makeup in the sun visor mirror.

"It's not terrible," I tell her. "It's just not what I thought I'd be doing."

Mom nods. "I understand, Lou," she says, and I feel an unfair stab of temper.

"Pfft. *Do* you?" I snark.

She raises an eyebrow at me and rolls her eyes in Dad's direction. Oh, right. I doubt anyone imagines they'll be roommates with their ex-husband. I smile a "sorry" at her.

I kiss them both and slide out of the car, followed by Lav. And now we're strangers again for the rest of the day. Although maybe not—surprisingly, she walks alongside me until we're halfway across the yard, before nudging me goodbye with her elbow and peeling off to sit with some friends. It's not much, but it feels sweet.

chapter 8

as I walk into school, I can hear the bell ringing for the beginning of afternoon classes. I check my schedule. Come on, P.E. . . . Please, please, P.E. The only class I don't find completely baffling.

Unless there's a new class called Lying Down and Having a Little Bit of Rest.

It's biology. Gutted.

I get there first and sit on a tall stool at the back. This is the best desk in the classroom—closest to the window, farthest from the teacher, good view of the tadpoles. Prime real estate! Someone will *have* to sit next to me.

You'd think. Everyone enters in gaggles of twos and threes, and they sit somewhere they can all be together. Melia comes in and I smile at her. But Cammie is right behind her. She spots me and mutters, "Tragic." The two girls with them laugh. Melia doesn't laugh, but she doesn't return my smile either.

Biology actually passes quickly, since I spend the whole class thinking about my hatred of Cammie, which is strong and healthy.

I get lost in daydreams of how happy I'd be if she got horrendous acne.

As we leave biology, I overhear Melia and her friends talking—apparently they're got a swim meet tonight, so the whole team is leaving right after school in the minibus.

Interesting.

At the end of school I watch the swim team congregate in the parking lot. Debs counts them all off, and they stick their sports bags and the box of packed dinners in the minibus trunk. Ah, that brings back memories of cheese rolls that always tasted of gas fumes.

I grab Lav and ask her to tell Dad I'll walk home, since I'll be a little bit late.

"Should I tell him you've got detention?" she asks.

"Yeah. He won't believe it, but go on."

I've never been in trouble at school. I don't think some of my teachers could pick me out of a lineup.

I put my hand in my bag and feel something silky. Excellent.

Everyone races past, happy to get out of school ASAP. If I were a teacher, I'd be a little hurt by how desperate my pupils were to leave. It's like they're fleeing a fire.

I walk against the tide, feeling a little thrill. I'm looking forward to this.

The swimming pool seems deserted, but I'm not risking it. I check all the changing stalls and even the toilets. With the exception of the occasional staff member wandering around, I have the whole place to myself.

My bathing suit is a little tighter than it used to be. I poke my stomach, I suspect that's the culprit. But as Mom always says when

Lav complains about her weight, "Some people don't have arms or legs! So shut up!"

Can't really argue with that.

I stride toward the swimming pool and I'm about to dive in when I notice that Pete, Roman, and his brother are loitering in the field *again*. They're kicking a soccer ball around, and Pete is definitely smoking.

If I had to name the person I find least relaxing to be around, I'd say Pete and Cammie are currently fighting for the top spot. But this is more my pool than the boys' so I'm determined to ignore them. They'll get bored and go away soon.

I dive in just from the side and it feels amazing. I swim a length and feel the muscles in my ribs stretching. Then I lie on my back in a starfish shape and scull gently, with small movements of my hands, just enough to spin me in a slow circle.

I take a deep breath and let it out bit by bit as I sink to the bottom of the pool, where I start somersaulting slowly, forward, then backward. I can feel the air in my nose—enough pressure to stop water from shooting up my nose but not enough to release any bubbles.

I don't know what this is that I'm doing at the bottom of the pool, but I've always been good at it. It's a useless trick, really, only good for making people think you've drowned. (If you need that skill regularly, then your life is more depressing than mine, and I tip my hat to you.)

I start to feel an ache in my ribs and I surface slowly, with my eyes closed. Mmmm. So relaxing.

I open my eyes.

Roman, Small Roman, and Pete are all standing at the side of the pool, looking down on me. In both ways, I sense

The silence hangs. I say weakly, "No outdoor shoes."

"What?" says Roman.

"Nothing."

Small Roman definitely heard what I said. He's like three feet closer to me than the other two.

"What were you doing down there?" asks Roman.

"Uh . . ."

Really, are we going to talk like this? I never usually feel naked in a bathing suit, but suddenly I do. I don't get out of the pool. I bob around, a little talking, floating idiot head.

I realize I need to give Roman more of an answer than "uh."

"Just floating around, really—somersaults and stuff."

"You a swimmer?" asks Pete.

I hesitate.

"Used to be. Don't do it anymore."

They all nod and Small Roman smiles at me. They have no idea what a massive big deal it was for me to say that.

"Do you swim?" I ask. They don't, of course, or I'd know them. But still, Operation: Make Friends is going surprisingly well here; let's not derail it.

"No, we're dancers" says Small Roman. Pete rolls his eyes.

"What?" protests Small Roman good-humoredly. "We still *are*!"

"What's this?" I ask. (Lav taught me the trick to talking to boys: not too many words. It looks eager. Treat everything you say like a tweet—140 characters or fewer.)

"OK, so for years we've been, like, this dance . . . uh . . ."

57

"Troupe?" I suggest.

"Collective," Pete corrects me. OK.

Small Roman goes on. "And we just auditioned for *Britain's Hidden Talent* but didn't even make it through to tryouts."

"I thought everyone tried out in front of the judges?" I asked.

"No," says Small Roman. "They're holding public auditions once a week for the next few months. We did the first one and got nowhere. You only get on TV if you're talented or mental. The people in the middle who are just deluded and a bit pathetic get sent home."

He looks so sad my heart breaks a little, and I scoop the water around me to fill the silence, which makes me spin in a small circle. "I'm sorry," I say sincerely once I'm facing him again.

"Apparently people are 'over' dance collectives now that there've been like a million of them on TV," explains Roman, scuffing his shoe along the floor tiles. "They said Gabe would appeal to young girls, but it didn't help."

"Uh-huh," I say, sneaking a glance at Small Roman. Who I guess is called Gabe and would be appealing if I weren't looking straight up his nose. My neck hurts.

"So we thought maybe something to do with swimming?" Gabe continues.

"Can you swim?" I ask. It seems a reasonable question unless they want to go on TV wearing water wings.

"Everyone can swim," scoffs Pete.

I'm about to argue with him about that, but Gabe jumps in. "We were playing soccer outside and . . ."

". . . we thought you'd drowned," adds Roman, in a way that makes me feel dumb.

"But when we came in, we saw you doing that amazing under-water acrobatics," says Gabe. "It's cool."

Roman and Pete nod and I feel a bit giddy with neck ache and compliments.

"So . . . teach us that?" says Roman.

"I don't want to be on TV," I lie. I do, I totally do, but holding my gold Olympic swimming medal and smiling modestly and tearfully at the cameras. Not prancing about in front of booing weirdos.

"Not *you*," says Roman bluntly. "You could train *us*."

"In . . . what, though? What *is* this?"

At this they all look extremely uncomfortable. They glance at each other, and I take the opportunity to stretch my neck down.

Ah ah ah aaaah. The pain is so intense I see spots of light. By the time I look up again, I think my eyes must be bulging like a squeezed hamster. I imagine. I've never squeezed a hamster, though Hannah did once when we were eight and I didn't stop her.

(Before you get all judge-y, Mr. Nibbles went on to live a full and happy life. For nine more days.)

"I guess it's kind of like . . . synchronized swimming," says Roman with an effort, and they all look like they're sucking a lemon. I try not to laugh. Poor boys, it must be so hard being cool all the time, eh?

"There was a synchronized swimming team from around here who got through last week's audition," says Gabe.

"But they were all girls and really hot," Pete remarks, suddenly enthusiastic.

"So hot," adds Roman, entirely unnecessarily, in my opinion.

Good for them. I smooth my wet hair behind my ears before I realize how that looks. *Insecuuuure!*

"So, you want me to train you?" I ask. Because although it is lovely to talk to boys about "hot" girls, I am getting very cold.

"Yeah. We can't pay you, though, we're broke," says Pete. From where I'm floating I'm exactly eye-level with his £150 Nike sneakers, and I allow myself a skeptical face.

"But we'll say hi to you at school," says Roman.

I stop treading water and sink a bit. I keep my chin underwater—my eyes feel very hot.

"*Duuude*," Gabe says quietly. Somehow that just makes me feel worse.

I can feel myself blushing; I swim away from them and hoist myself out of the pool on the other side. I can hear murmuring behind me. I know they're discussing whether I'm upset (YES) or maybe even crying. (NO. That is water from the pool on my face. Yes, all of it.)

I *may* be a social outcast (fine, I *am*), but I don't deserve this. It's mean, and I've had a gutful of people being mean. I wanted to come and swim without Cammie and her bitchy friends, and instead I run into the male version.

Plus, in my mind, I'm already telling Hannah this story later, and I want to tell her how I left in a haughty silence, so that is what I do.

chapter 9

fantastic dramatic exit, Lou. Except . . . in the locker room I realize I didn't bring a towel with me, so I have to dab myself dry with toilet paper. Twenty-five minutes later, picking damp tissue clumps off my legs, I head out of the sports center.

Why is everything so hard? I want one thing to go right. Please, just one thing. I kick the door open, and it doesn't bounce back and smash me in the face and knock all my teeth out. This is a start, though I was looking for more, TBH.

I look around. You have to be careful when you walk home alone. It's starting to get dark. I check my watch. I really didn't mean to be this late.

I've never stayed out late and lied about where I was before. I was hardly boozing at a bus stop, but still I'm impressed by my new rebellious behavior. For a newbie, I've really committed to it; in fact, I've done overtime!

Typical dweeb. Lav'll love that.

When I get in, Mom and Lav are crashed in front of the TV. They look up at me, and from their faces, I guess it's obvious I had cried as I jogged. I scoop some tears out of my ear.

"How's my goldfish?" asks Mom, patting the sofa beside her. She doesn't realize what she's just called me—my nickname from all the gold medals I used to bring home. Not because I *once* pooped in the pool on a holiday to Spain when I was five, despite what Laverne may say.

I sit beside Mom, slide down, and put my head on her shoulder. When I stretch my aching legs out, they go past Mom's feet. She nudges them with her knees. "So leggy" she tuts. That's nice.

We watch TV for a little while. Funnily enough, it's *Britain's Hidden Talent*. I've never really paid attention to it before. The stage is huge, and the contestants look tiny on it—I'd be terrified if that were me. There are lights zigzagging all over it, and the sort of music that gets you excited in the pit of your stomach. It seems a little less bizarre that three of the coolest boys I know would be into it.

A hefty man wearing only gold underpants prances onto the stage. Nope, *still* bizarre.

I can see it would be cool to be on that stage if you were doing something impressive, though swimming underwater wouldn't have been my first thought. How would you even get a swimming pool up there?

Boys, I think with an amused weariness. Like I've got any idea about boys.

"There's pasta in the kitchen," says Mom, and I go and help myself.

"How was school?" she shouts through to me.

"Yeah. Hmmm. How was your date last night?"

"Yeah. Hmmm. Oh, that reminds me. Mark!"

"Yeah?" Dad shouts from upstairs. I roll my eyes. Mom never thinks that three people in three different rooms is a reason *not* to chat.

"You know Laura who I work with?"

"No, but OK?"

"She asked me if you were single!"

Pause.

"And if I'd give her your number so she could call you."

That's so complicated. See, even old people need Facebook.

There's a silence from upstairs. Then he shouts down, "Is Laura the pretty redhead?"

Mom and Dad are a little frosty with each other for the rest of the night. Lav and I make our excuses early and head to bed, where I tell Hannah what happened today at the pool—which is really lengthy by text. She texts back immediately: Hey, at least you're talking to boys, right?

Always the optimist.

There are some dots on my screen—she's still typing.

Are you annoyed at them? she asks.

Yes, I reply honestly.

So . . . technically, you're having BOY TROUBLE.

Ooh. That's one way of looking at it. I imagine myself at school tomorrow, looking weary, knocking back a coffee and saying to a passing upperclassman, "Men! Am I right?"

The next morning Dad drops us off early, probably trying to get back into Mom's good graces. As we're leaving, she says he should keep an eye out for our geography teacher, the *pretty redhead*. Zing.

"Good luck with your job interview today," I say as I get out of the car and give him a kiss. Lav gives him a fist bump.

Poor Dad, I wish I could do his interviews for him. I'd be terrible at them. He's a project manager, and I can't even manage my socks into pairs, but I want to protect him from any more rejection.

I jog up the front steps of school, past kids enjoying the sunshine before they go in. I look up, and catch Gabe's eye. Of course, he's my sister's year. I don't know why I've never seen him before, though.

"Hi," he says.

"OK," I say.

Yes, I know. *Hi* is the word I was looking for. No one replies to "hi" with "OK." Except this social moron.

I carry on up the steps past Gabe, pushing my Boy Trouble from my mind, and head to English, just to double-check how little I know about *that* subject.

I can read and write, so it could be worse. And actually I read a lot over the summer because I had nothing else to do, so this lesson isn't too bad. Which is nice, since Mr. Peters is our English teacher and I'm glad that he can see there's more to me than crying on the floor, covered in tampons.

At lunchtime I attempt to chat in the lunch line with a girl I recognize from my homeroom. "Oh great, macaroni and cheese!" I say. Come on, how could this go wrong?

She gives me a startled look. "It's basically nothing but carbs and fat. You know that, right?"

"Well," I say, feeling we'd headed in a direction I hadn't expected, "you need some carbohydrates and fat to live."

"No, you don't" she tells me firmly, "I've got an app for that."

So she's not going to be my new friend—I think we both feel

that. I find an empty table near the garbage to eat alone. I act like my bread roll is fascinating, "Oh, so it's bread *all the way around?* I never knew."

After a few minutes a girl in the grade above approaches me and loiters by my table, looking effortlessly cool. She has a tan and is wearing tons of little delicate necklaces and bracelets that jingle when she moves.

She stands, jingling.

I sit, holding my bread roll.

"Hey," she says, like it's a bit of an effort.

I try to seem even less fussed. Well, if that's the game we're playing! Maybe I'll fall asleep midsentence.

She holds a piece of paper out toward me, subtly, between two fingers, as if she's working undercover.

I stare at it. Why is she passing me a note? She raises her sculpted eyebrows at me like I'm being weird. I'm not being weird! You're being weird! I take the note from her and she drifts away.

I'm tempted to put the note in the garbage and forget about it, but Lav says I have to be less suspicious of people at school; some of them might be nice. *I* say, pelt me with tampons once, shame on you. Pelt me twice, shame on me. Pelt me three times, and this is why we're banned from Walmart.

Who would pass me a note, though? Unless it's Carbs Girl with a warning about this bread roll. Oh, fine, I'll read it. But if it's mean, I'm *demanding* homeschooling.

Hi, this is the guy from the swimming pool yesterday.
The one with the rude brother. I'm sorry Roman upset
you, that was stupid—I sent a messenger in case you

don't want to talk to any of us. Can we try again? I get
that it seems weird but this means a lot to us. We've
been dancing together since we were kids and we'd love
to be on TV together. And I think you could be the person
to help us. How about £20 a session? Know it's not much,
but it's all we've got—and a plus-one to the *BHT* final?!

Gabriel

Ha. Gabriel and Roman, someone's parents knew they had a
couple of winners on their hands, didn't they?

My pride is still bruised, and why does he assume I like *BHT*?
What is up with that? You don't just assume everyone likes mud
wrestling, do you? (I bet watching mud wrestling is a lot less upset-
ting than watching an underdressed woman dance with her over-
dressed dog.)

But twenty quid. I do need money. I'm never going to become
more socially acceptable if I always dress like I've got the flu. Dad
can't give me any while he hasn't got a job, and I bet Mom has higher
bills now that there are four of us (and one is busy dismantling everything we own).

Gabriel put his phone number at the bottom, so I save it to my
contacts, which now has *three* boys in it (though the other two are
related to me).

I text him: OK, when do you want to meet? It looks pretty unfriendly, but then I don't want to sound too excited—I'm remembering Lav's rule. I hover my thumb over my phone, debating how
to make it a bit nicer. Maybe an emoji? Probably not the poo with a
smile, though it's pretty multipurpose. . . .

Too late! My thumb accidentally hits Send and I watch my

unfriendly message whoosh away. He replies immediately. I would've waited a while to look unfussed, but he doesn't even bother to pretend.

Great! Tomorrow, 7 at the pool?

Cool. It's a date. Or, you know . . . something that couldn't be less like a date if it tried.

chapter 10

Weeez! I cannot BELIEVE you're a swimming coach! Are you the new Debs? Are you wearing teeny tiny shorts? When the wind blows do you feel it in your kidneys? That's how you know they're too small. I'm terrified about what I'm going to come home to. New news, they get us to eat raw fish here, it's gross!! Like eating the inside of your mouth. You gotta try it, no calories and all protein apparently. Hashtag fact of the day and you're welcome.

Han x

aargh! It's my first underwater training thingy in half an hour and Mom's thrown all my clothes in the wash. Why does she do this? I run to the laundry basket in the bathroom. Nothing in there, so I hurry back to my (*our*) bedroom, keeping a tight grip on my towel, as it's currently the only outfit I've got. Maybe with the right shoes I can style it out.

Lav is lying on her bed, flicking through a magazine so shiny it's bouncing light around the room.

"Laaaaav?"

She looks up but doesn't take her earbuds out.

"Please can I borrow something to wear? I've got to get to my . . . job."

She languidly pulls out one earbud. "You have a job? Cool! But of course you can't borrow my clothes. Best of luck with everything."

"No, no, please!" I say before she puts her earbud back in. "Not your nice clothes, obviously, just like some sports stuff . . ."

"Sports stuff?" she says, as if she's never heard these words before but suspects they're dirty.

"Something you'd sleep in but I'd wear out," I explain.

"Oh. Yeah, third drawer down."

She hesitates. "Your hair?"

"Yes?"

If she says the word pubic, *I. Will. Cry.*

"Come here," she says, reaching onto her shelf for a jar of oil. She pours a little drop into her hands, stands in front of me, and starts smoothing it gently through my hair. This is all very surprising.

"Thanks, Lav, this is . . . nice of you.

"It's good to see you cheer up, instead of lying on your bed, pretending you're not crying."

"Sorry about that."

"I was going to start hanging fairy lights off you to lighten the mood, but I thought you'd electrocute yourself with tears."

I stand silently while she massages oil into my hair. Hannah and

I used to make fun of Lav behind her back for being a ditzy "boy-centric," as a teacher once said. But if this last week has taught me anything, it's that I am *not* the brains of the family.

My head and face burn hot, and the rubbing isn't really helping. It's like Lav is determined to bring all my shame out in one massive blush.

"Thank you!" I say, pulling away from her before my head explodes.

"That's OK," she says. "We'll figure out your hair this week, then work on your skin."

She has a way of making me feel like an old car she's going to fix up.

I run downstairs and out the front door, hearing Mom call something as I slam it behind me. It didn't sound like "Good luck." Oh no, wait, it was "Don't slam the door."

Whoopsy.

I run down the road and up the embankment toward the swimming pool. The number of times I've run this route, I could get there with my eyes closed, though I don't try it. I don't want to get hit by a car before Lav's "worked on" my skin.

Life is full of surprises, I muse, and a sudden draft around my midriff proves me right. My top doesn't reach my trousers. This is the last time I borrow Lav's clothes.

As I run, I feel an unfamiliar sensation. . . . It's my hair bouncing! It's never bounced. *Crunched*, maybe.

I round the corner, hurdle over a few flower beds, and burst into the swimming pool to the sound of cheering. I wheel around to see what I've interrupted. Is there a race on? But no, it's the three boys, cheering *me*!

"Here she is!" announces Gabriel.

That is such a great way to enter a room. I beam. Then I dial the beam down a little. Don't be too eager, Louise. Be cool.

I cough. I am *cool*.

"See you at the bottom," says Roman, pulling his tracksuit off. I am so pathetic I blush. (Roman said "bottom" to me! Ha ha. I'll tell Han.)

"Not yet!" I assert, fiddling with my backpack to hide my blush. "I need to see how strong you are as swimmers before we start doing anything underwater."

"Why?" says Pete brusquely.

I look at him hard. Maybe it's the run, maybe it's the fact that my hair bounced, or maybe it's the cheering, but I feel some of my old confidence return.

"Because while some people like to believe that 'anyone' can swim, they are, in fact, wrong."

Pete doesn't say anything but looks like he's biting back a nasty remark.

"And, sorry, I don't know your name . . . ?" (I do know his name. I am being extremely petty, but it's *fun*. And I haven't been splashing around in much fun lately—I deserve it.)

"Pete."

"OK, *Pete*," I say, bouncing a little on the balls of my feet and feeling like a mini-Debs. I can see Gabriel stifling a smirk behind him. "I'm Lou and I'm in charge of you while we're in this pool. And I don't want you to drown. So I need you to show me that you can swim. Please."

Pete sighs and slides into the water.

"I've been swimming for years," he scoffs. "I'm probably faster

71

than you. Don't get weird about it, but men are stronger than women, you have to admit."

"Excuse me," I tell him, and grab my backpack and head for the locker room. As I push through the door, I can hear Gabriel say, "Stop being rude to her. If she goes, we don't have anyone else."

I march back out of the locker room a few minutes later wearing my bathing suit. I step up on the diving block and look down at them. "Four lengths, front crawl?" I snap on my swimming cap.

"Uh . . ." Gabe begins.

"Nope!" I beam at him. "Time to race."

They all step up on diving blocks beside me and I nod at the minute clock.

"Let's go on twelve." I watch the second hand slide toward the top, and then I dive, hard. It feels a little unfamiliar, sensations you forget about, like the feel of water slapping against your armpit. . . . I'm slower these days, but still faster than three cocky civilians. Probably. *Hopefully.*

I start to feel winded on the final length, but I think of Pete scoffing at me and I push onward. I slap my hands against the side of the pool and lift my head. I'm aware that no one is next to me, and I get a stomach-lurching fear that they finished ages ago and are already out of the pool, playing keepy-uppy with a float or texting their girlfriends. Unsportspersonlike!

But I hear splashing behind me, and my stomach unknots. After a few long seconds, Pete slaps his hands down beside me, Roman a second later on the other side. Roman, panting hard, looks genuinely impressed. Pete even manages a rueful "whatever" shrug. I smile. Normal service has resumed.

We turn around, wiping water out of our eyes and ears, and

watch Gabriel swimming toward us. He's just started the final length—he's not a bad swimmer, but he's slow and clearly exhausted. I don't feel like being cocky anymore.

"He's been ill," says Roman suddenly.

"What?"

"Gabriel. He had ME for years. You know, myalgic encephalomyelitis?"

"Is that when you're tired all the time?"

"Yeah. Sometimes he didn't leave the house for months."

So that's why I hadn't seen him before.

"It's amazing he's back in school, but he's not very fit," Roman goes on.

This is an understatement. We have time for quite a lengthy medical conversation while Gabriel finishes the race.

"Is this going to be OK?" Roman says, looking from Gabriel to me as if I have all the answers.

"Yes," I lie.

I don't know what they're trying to do. I don't know if it's even got a name or if it's just Drowning to Music. But I'm involved now, and as I watch Gabriel swim his final lap, I know I'll do whatever I can to make this work for him. Them, I mean.

Gabriel reaches the edge and staggers to his feet. He can't breathe; he's red in the face, but he's smiling. "You have no idea, but that's good for me," he pants.

"That's good for me too," I lie. I'm getting better with practice. "Easily good enough! Yep!"

chapter 11

We all dry off, put sweatshirts on, and have a talk about what they want to do. They show me some of their dance moves. If anyone walked in right now, it would look like they were showing off to try to impress me. Tragically, no one does.

People only walk in on me when I'm crying or picking up tampons, apparently.

The boys are really good—Pete and Roman can do a ton of strength holds and flips, and Gabriel is less strong but bendy and wiry. I can see them doing this as kids, Pete and Roman as best friends for years, letting Roman's little brother join in. Even Pete seems less intimidating when I imagine him as an eight-year-old landing on his head after another backflip turns into a back flop.

As they bounce around on their hands, it turns into a competition between Pete and Roman. I get the feeling most things do. I watch while their faces go redder, but they refuse to give up first, while Gabe stretches out a cramp.

"Did they say anything else . . . the tryout guys?" I ask, mainly to distract them so one of them will fall over and we can get back to training.

"Just that they had enough dancers," Pete says in an upside-down gasp.

Gabe and I look at each other, OK, it's not the most helpful advice.

"And," comes a voice from under Roman's sweatshirt, which is currently sliding down his torso and revealing . . . ahem, never mind. "They said that we had a strong look."

Pete slowly topples over into the water wings box.

"Careful!" I call over. "They're covered in wart remover strips."

Pete scrabbles out of the squeaking pile, making retching noises while Gabe and Roman laugh. I don't think I've ever been funny in front of someone who wasn't family or Hannah. I always feel hilarious *inside*, but the message never seems to get out.

"So . . ." Pete turns to me, rubbing his neck. "You don't know what you're doing, then?"

I stand up for myself. "Pete, dancing underwater isn't a Thing. I'm happy to help, but it's synchronized swimming without all that pesky breathing. Do you have any idea what you'll perform in?"

"Swimming trunks," says Gabe promptly. "Ideally?"

Pete ignores this, though it makes Roman laugh.

"My dad works at the aquarium," Pete says, like it's obvious. "They have these spare tanks, and we're going to borrow one."

"OK," I say slowly. "By 'spare' you mean . . ."

"In an unlocked warehouse."

"And by 'borrow' you mean . . ."

"Well . . ."

"*Steal?*"

"Don't be dramatic."

"Well, I can't see any problem with that plan at all. Great stuff."

I rub my stomach, which has clenched hard at that news. Like I don't have enough to worry about. An ill swimmer, a grumpy one, and one I'm too shy to look at; a sport I think we're inventing on the spot; a local team already through to the final (and they're "really hot," so woo for them) . . .

. . . and now we'll be performing in a stolen tank that's probably full of old fish poop.

I reach for my phone to Google *illnesses from fish poop?*

"Sorry?" Pete is looking pointedly at my phone. "Do you have time for that?"

He's right. *Rude* but right. I need to concentrate—we have a *lot* to do.

The boys slide back into the water, and I put thoughts of fish poo to one side. I've made a playlist for their training sessions. I was up all night choosing songs that were cool but, you know, not too cool; not self-consciously cool. But still cool. (It was as exhausting as it sounds.)

I rub my tired eyes—they feel like boiled eggs—and pop my phone into Lav's portable speakers. (I did ask her permission. Very quietly . . . when she was in another room.)

"I made a playlist, guys!" I announce to the group. It's hard teaching people who intimidate you. You find yourself calling them "guys!" a lot. I press Play and get them to do some leg stretches while they tread water. I watch their faces for any early signs of sneering, but no one even mentions the music. It must be OK.

School has taught me that people make fun of you when something is lame and stay silent if it's acceptable.

"Hey," says Gabe, "you've got great taste in music."

"Thank you!" I casually push back my bangs in a gesture far more suited to Lav, but whatever.

I ask them to sink underwater a little to see if they can lie a foot beneath the surface without panicking. Most people struggle with that. Roman and Gabriel get it quickly, but Pete is a massive control freak and keeps thrashing around. I tell him it's really hard to master, which seems to wave a flag on a temporary truce between us.

While they're practicing sinking, I get dressed and then come back to stand at the side of the pool. I have the guys treading water and lifting their arms up to test their strength and, yes, *maybe* I have found a whistle and *perhaps* it does give me a mild feeling of power. But it's the only way to get their attention when they're underwater. Honest!

Suddenly the doors bang open and Debs strides into the pool area. (Can't she ever just *walk* anywhere? And put some pants on.)

I look down at the outfit I borrowed from Lav—it's about as small as what Debs is wearing. This is my new look: half-naked stalker. I quickly hide my whistle under my T-shirt, not that it offers much coverage.

Debs is followed by Cammie, Melia, and two other girls I know from swimming, Nicole and Amanda. If I were that pretty (and I can't lie—they all look like a shampoo ad), I think I could find it in my heart to be a nice person. But Cammie, Nicole, and Amanda are all actively mean—not just to me, to everyone. Melia is neutral; she doesn't stop them, but she isn't horrible herself. I'm not sure if that makes her a good person.

The boys immediately drop their arms and start swimming around like they're just having a casual swim, nothing to see here, no biggie, guys. Which is great, except now I'm standing on the edge of the pool *watching them* like a total weirdo.

"Hey, Pete," says Cammie archly.

"All right," he replies.

"Not bad," she sighs, totes unfussed.

The three girls watch this incredibly boring back-and-forth with looks on their faces like, "What's going on here? Cammie and her exciting love life, eh?"

Debs takes in the scene, a wry smile on her face. "OK, Louise?"

"Yes, thank you, Deb-o-rah," I say tightly.

"Just watching boys, are you?"

Debs looks down at my outfit, and her lips move as if she's about to say something but refrains. She's got that Pete thing, where you always think a withering put-down is just around the corner. It's so unnerving, like being trapped in a car with a wasp.

Would I have ended up like that if I'd got through to the Olympic training? Is Hannah going to? It makes me glad I didn't get . . . hmm . . .

No, if I'm honest with myself, I'd still rather be a horrible cow with a gold medal. I could always go into therapy later, sort myself out.

"Are you *coaching* them for something, Lou? Good, good, fill the days."

"Coaching them?" I ask, stuffing down my rage and faking complete confusion. "For what?" Debs's eyes narrow.

"So what *are* you doing?" she asks carefully.

"Just swimming," says Gabe, and swims a little circle to demonstrate. He is a terrible liar. We'll leave him at home the night we steal a fish tank.

Debs still looks suspicious.

I panic and say, "I'm just hanging out here out of habit, really, I miss swimming." Apparently the best lies have a grain of truth in them. There's a silence. I know Debs so well—she hates emotional stuff.

She keeps walking toward her office, followed by the four girls, and I feel a temporary sense of victory. She's backing down, she's leaving us alone! This is amazing! Take that, Debs, you and your stupid girl gang. She shuts the door like a full stop.

I turn back to the boys with my most unbothered face.

"*Pfft*. Don't even know why they're here. There's no swim practice tonight."

"No," says Pete, hanging off the side of the pool and readjusting his goggles. "That's the swimming team that's already through."

Hot vomit jumps at my ribs.

"What, the *BHT* team?" I croak, feeling my Unbothered Face fall off. Now, where's my Extremely Bothered Face . . . ?

"Yeah."

"Argyhjfffgggg."

"You OK, Lou?"

"I am *fine*. Everything is *fine*. When's the next public tryout?"

"This weekend."

"*This* weekend?!" Here's my Extremely Bothered Face—I'm wearing it.

"Yeah," says Gabriel calmly. "It's up north. There are weeks more tryouts, and it's another five weeks before they come back to this part of the country, so it's cool."

Depends on your definition of *cool*.

"Five weeks isn't very long," I grumble.

"Well, it's a hundred quid to you," says Roman reasonably.

"Are you paying me per session or per week?" I ask cheekily. Pete and Roman look at me stony-faced. Gabe watches this with mild curiosity.

"Because the note said per session . . ."

They say nothing.

"Per week it is, then," I agree. (Wooohoo! A hundred quid!) "Seems reasonable," I chat mildly to myself as I pack up my sports bag. (Wheeeeeeee! *That's so much money!*)

"Are you going, then, now that you've earned your money for today?" asks Roman. I can't tell if he's teasing or serious.

"I'm not allowed out past nine on a weeknight. My dad's coming to get me," I say honestly.

Pete and Roman seem to find that funny, but I don't know why.

"So between now and the next session you'll come up with a routine?" says Roman. Somehow he manages to make it sound more like an order than a question.

"Ab-so-*lute*ly." I give him a big, fake, calm smile.

An . . . underwater synchronized swimming routine. Yes. I'll just come up with one of them, then. *Easy.*

"I'll work out a routine, and then we'll try it next time we meet, and hopefully you won't drown."

Gabriel laughs, Roman smiles, Pete ignores me.

chapter 12

he boys stop to get something from the vending machine, and I don't want to look socially clingy, so I go wait outside. My phone dings, a message from Hannah:

Get outta town. Did YOU know bananas were fattening?!
I LIVE OFF BANANAS! ☹

Dad pulls up in Mom's car.

"*Dad!*"

"What?"

"You know *full well* what."

He's just wearing pajama shorts with a coat thrown over the top. He even has his slippers on.

"I look normal from the outside," he says. "You can only tell if you're right next to the car and look in and down."

"Bye, Lou," say Roman, Pete, and Gabriel as they walk right past the car, looking in and down.

"Oh dear." Dad grins. "Have I made you look uncool?"

"*Yes*, actually," I tell him, "so don't smirk at me like it's no big deal, because that's exactly what you've done. I have zero friends at school, two and a half acquaintances" (given the mild hostility bubbling off Pete, I won't consider him a whole acquaintance) "and you just embarrassed me in front of them. So you can stop smiling about it."

"Louise, being popular isn't about trying to be cool," says Dad.

He has *no* idea how wrong he is. This is exactly the sort of terrible, awful, useless advice you get from people over twenty-five. I've heard it a million times, along with how I'll be pretty when I'm older and one day I'll regret shaving my legs. (When? When I want to stuff a duvet cheaply and need all that thick leg fur? I *don't* think so.)

"You know, being popular," says the Man Who Doesn't Get It, warming to his theme, "it's about doing what *you* like."

Why doesn't he just tell me to be myself?

"Just be yourself," he goes on, nonsense spouting out of his head. "Do what makes you happy, and then everyone will see how cool you are and want to be friends with *you*!"

"Okaaaay! Thank you so much, Dad. I really appreciate that you care, especially since you have so much on your plate at the moment. But this is terrible advice. Being cool is *not* about being yourself, it's *not*, and you need to stop handing out that advice in case one day someone actually listens to you and you ruin their life. I *am* myself and I have *one* friend, who emails me details of meals. And my school days are *so* lonely and it's not fun. You have no idea what it's like to be lonely. I'm sorry, but no."

There's a silence.

"It's lonely being unemployed," says Dad.

I rub my finger along the door handle and stare at the chocolate wrappers on the floor.

He takes a deep breath. "You wake up and you have nowhere to go and everyone rushes off to school and work, where people notice if they're not there and where people need them, while I sit at home and email people asking them to notice me or need me and no one does. That's unemployment. If you don't like school, Louise, at least it will end soon and you'll make new friends somewhere else. But *I* don't know when this will end."

We stop at some traffic lights. On impulse I grab Dad's hand.

"*We* need you," I tell him. "Me and Lav and Mom. We all need you and we like having you around. Look, you and Mom are divorced and she's still happy to live with you. Think how amazing that makes you! And I have to share a room with Lav and all her girl . . . smells . . . and glitter that gets *everywhere* and spiky boot things and I'm still happier that you're here."

"Thanks, Lou," he says.

My palm sweats gently.

"Should we stop holding hands now, Dad?"

"Yeah, I need to change gear."

Someone behind us beeps loudly. The light has turned green.

"Do you mind?" Dad yells. "We're bonding and we're new to it!!"

We drive home in silence. But a nice silence.

I text Hannah:

Then why aren't monkeys fat?

chapter 13

8:48
Hey guys, we're all going to hang out before the swimming
tournament next weekend, if the weather's nice we'll go to
that park near the leisure center—let's all meet at the fountain
at 1?

Cammie xx

8:51
Sorry, Lou! I forgot to take you off the group email for the swim
team! Ignore this, see ya round.

Cx

the next morning is Saturday and Mom is making eggy bread.
She calls it French toast, but I can't see why dipping something in
egg makes it French. It puts me off the idea of French fries. I share
this thought with the kitchen.

"Yes, and French letters," agrees Mom. Dad laughs explosively. Lav and I frown and Google that on our phones.

"Ew, Mooom . . ." says Lav, who has 4G. I have 3G, so it takes me longer to be grossed out. But it still happens.

"Dad was saying you've made some new friends," says Mom brightly. Thanks, Dad.

"Well." I summarize it for her. "I am employed by three people too cool to be my actual friends."

"Oh, come on!" she scoffs. "My Lou doesn't care what people think of her." So very incorrect.

"No, I just dress badly. Which makes it look like I don't care, but I do. If I had some cash, I'd buy some new clothes and then you could see how badly I care about what people think of me."

Lav nods, backing me up, then returns to her phone.

"Not that I need cash," I say hastily, for Dad's sake. "Because material things like money aren't as important as, like, family and love and that. Plus I'm earning twenty quid a week coaching these three."

"I can't believe you've got a job before me!" says Dad, poking me in the shoulder. "What are you coaching them in?"

"Burlesque," I tell him. He blinks at me. "*Swimming*, obviously!"

"That's nice. I bet you're good at that. So, your new friends. What are their naaames?" Mom persists.

"My *employers* are Roman, Gabriel, and Pete," I give in and tell them.

"What?" says Lav, putting down her phone. "How are you friends with *them*?" She suddenly realizes how rude that sounds. "No, I mean . . . the thing is . . . OK, ha, what that *sounded* like . . ."

"I know, Lav, I'm just helping them out with something."

"You should get them to say hi to you at school, though," she says. "If people think you know them, you'll have a better chance of making some friends. That's why Becky used to play cards with Pete's gran when she did work placement at the residential care home."

"Laverne! That's a terrible thing to say!" exclaims Mom.

We both look at her and try to work out which part she means.

"No, Mom, it's true," I say. "Now that Hannah's gone, I don't have anyone to hang out with."

"Which is not her fault," Lav informs Mom.

"It is a *little*," I say gloomily.

"Why don't you 'hang out' with each other?" Mom asks.

We look at her as if she's suggested we grow tails.

"Anyway, it's because you always had Hannah," Lav continues. "You didn't know she'd just disappear one day to Swim Team School."

"High Performance Training Camp," I correct her, but quietly.

"And school is stupid." She looks very adult all of a sudden. "You know who your school friends are?"

"Invisible Girl and Nonexistent Boy."

She ignores this. "They're people who *happen* to be your age who *happen* to live near you. So you end up in the same class, and that's who you've got to choose from. Just sit tight a few more years, and then there's a whole world out there of people you'll like more."

We all sit and digest that.

"Well," says Mom, "Lou has a job and Laverne's become a philosopher." She looks at Dad and shrugs. "I guess our work is done. I don't know about you, but I'm going to hang around outside Mickey D's and take selfies."

"Nice for some," says Dad, getting up from the table. "I've got to get my nails done for prom and I have literally *nothing* to wear!"

Lav and I roll our eyes. They think they're so funny.

"I don't take selfies," I inform them sniffily.

"Yes," says Lav, not really helping, "and I don't wear acrylics. They're so bad for your natural nails."

chapter 14

Lou

Guys, click on the link, could we do this move?

Pete

I could.

Roman

We could if we had gills. Seriously, Lou?

Lou

Sorry, sorry, just a thought.

Pete

Are you having trouble with the routine?

Lou

No!! Course not, no. LOL.

Gabe

Hey guys, what did I miss? I was washing my gills.

Lou

Ha ha.

Gabe

Don't make fun of my gills.

roman creates a WhatsApp group for me, him, Pete, and Gabe. When it first popped up on my phone, I was sitting in the cafeteria by myself and I went bright red. Cammie would kill to be Whats-Apping Pete and Roman every day. If only she *knew*. Ha!

I hug my smugness to myself, wishing everyone knew.

I watch her, holding court at her table of girls, her shiny pony-tail swooshing with every overdramatic gesture. She feels me look-ing at her and turns her head to fix me with a challenging stare. She mouths at me: "Stop staring at me, you lesbian."

I go red again and return to being *very* interested in my lunch. *Aha, Ms. Bread Roll, we meet again.*

Forget Cammie. I still feel smug. Though less smug when Roman and Gabe walk past and completely and utterly ignore me. I look up at them with a friendly smile that I turn into a cough, then a gri-mace, and finally some choking on bread.

So I sort of have friends, but they're secret friends, too ashamed to acknowledge me in public. Cool, cool, that's cool.

It's a tricky week. I spend every lunchtime and evening Googling synchronized swimming, but it all looks so boring. I wonder what Debs's team is doing, but I know there's no way I can spy on them. Cammie seems to have a Lou-radar. I spend most of my time try-ing, and failing, to be ignored by her.

Every time I finish on the school computer, I dump my cache. The last thing I need is to be outed as some sort of synchronized swimming obsessive. During lessons I doodle ideas in my notebook and try to think like Hannah—constant optimism! Maybe underwater synchronized swimming is a Thing. It's just a new Thing.

New things always look weird to begin with. Imagine being the first monkey who grew a thumb. No one realized how useful that was going to be. They probably all ran around yelling, "Look at Clive's hand! It's icky, hit it with a rock!" Thousands of years later, we're texting with it and Clive has the last laugh.

By the end of the week I'm so obsessed with synchronized swimming routines that at dinner I stick six green beans in a pile of mashed potatoes and imagine they're legs. I'm up all night with my phone in my mouth, using it as a flashlight so I can see my notebook as I scribble in it. Lav has made several two a.m. death threats, but I argue, quite reasonably, that now I'm frightened to turn the light off in case she sneaks up on me.

I don't have time to juggle everything, and I find I'm having this conversation a lot:

"Louise, where is your homework?"

"Ah . . . is it not in the pile on your desk?"

"No, because you didn't put it on my desk, so if it were on my desk, that would be spooky, wouldn't it?"

"Ha ha ha ha ha, that's funny, Mr. P. Great stuff."

"Louise?"

"Hello, yes?"

"GIVE. ME. YOUR. HOMEWORK."

Teachers always used to give me extra time to do my homework because, between training and traveling to competitions, I only had my morning breaks to scribble out something. Now I'm working even harder, but because it's secret, I have to do my homework too!

Not to sound like a Classic Teenager here, but seriously, *so* un-fair. Fascists

And I *am* trying. I hate being the densest person in my class. I stick my hand up for every question (I mainly get them wrong, but hey, good arm exercise, right?) and take tons of notes in class, even if my books are covered in long jagged scrawls from where I fall asleep midword.

A week after our first training session, I meet the boys for another one after school. They all seem pretty excited. Even Pete's eyes light up as I pull my big notebook out of my backpack, open it carefully, and hold it up for them to admire.

In places I've had to tape extra pages onto it to make a bigger canvas for my designs. I feel like a mad scientist unveiling some freakish experiment—"*Behold!* I have bent the laws of Nature to my own demonic will!" (*Maniacal cackling.*)

The boys stare at it in silence. I feel my smile falter. Do they not like it? Maybe it's not ambitious enough. Did I draw Gabriel too small? I should've just put *G*, *P*, and *R* on their heads.

Roman looks at me, opens his mouth, frowns, and closes it again. He goes back to scrutinizing the notepad.

"Lou," Pete says with typical grace and politeness, "what the f—?"

"It's amazing!" Gabriel jumps in loudly.

"Thanks." I beam at him.

"It's just . . . what is it?"

Really? I thought it was perfectly obvious. I take them through it patiently.

"Here's the three of you—"

"Am I the one with the big ears?" Pete interrupts.

"Yes."

"And I'm the little one?" Gabe says.

Definitely should've just put *G*, *R* and *P* over stick figures.

"Um, yes. Now this is the three of you doing a twist dive in from the side, then barreling down to the bottom, where you form a circle."

"Form a circle how?" asks Roman.

"Hold your ankles! Now, *here's* where it gets a tad tricky. . . ." I'm engrossed in my diagrams and only look up when I realize they're not crowding around my notebook. They're all bent double.

"Are you . . . ill?" I ask.

"I can't touch my toes!" gasps Gabe.

"Yours are a lot closer than mine, man," pants Pete.

Roman straightens up. "We can't touch our toes," he asserts, as if it's *my* fault.

"Really?"

"Well, touch yours, then," Pete challenges me.

I bend, wrap my fingers around my toes, and stand up. Honestly, call themselves dancers?

"Don't worry." I say. "Bodies are bendier in water."

"Are they?" Of course it's Pete who challenges me. I blow my whistle at him.

"Yes." (I have no idea.) "Everyone in the water and let's try it out!"

They line up along the edge of the pool, looking dubious. I stand on a bench and demonstrate a twist dive as best I can. They all nod.

"Three . . . two . . . one . . . DIVE!"

Let me say right here and now: I thought they could do this routine.

I swear I wasn't trying to make them look stupid, as Pete

suggests through a bloody tissue. (Roman kicked him in the face and caused a nosebleed.) I wasn't trying to kill anyone either, though I accept, if that had been my aim, I'd have been pretty happy with how the evening went.

But I'm not happy with it; I'm quietly devastated. I sit on a bench at the side of the pool as Pete lists the many reasons he wants this week's twenty quid back. He twists a tissue up his nose to leave both hands free for gesticulating. My stupidity demands a lot of hand gestures, apparently.

I bow my head and mutter "Sorry" every time Pete pauses for breath.

"All right, that's enough." I didn't notice Roman come back from the bathroom. He's finished throwing up now, after Gabe accidentally head-butted him in the stomach.

Gabe isn't unharmed either. I hadn't really factored in enough places to breathe, so he got dizzy and had to be fished out of the pool.

There's a silence, and I seize the opportunity. "I thought you were better swimmers!"

Three pairs of eyes swivel toward me. The mood isn't friendly.

"OK. I didn't mean it like I'm blaming you. I honestly thought it would be good. I'm really sorry."

My voice cracks and trails off. I feel a tear slip down my cheek.

"I can come up with an easier routine! I mean better one. A *better* one." I'm begging them now. No one is looking at me, not even Gabe. I pick up my backpack and head for the door.

I walk slowly, giving them time to calm down and stop bleeding and retching long enough to say it's OK and let's try again.

When I finally reach the door, *still* no one has said, "Come back,

Lou! Sorry we're lame swimmers! This is all our fault now that we think about it, but please could you give us an easier routine for our feeble abilities?"

First Debs, now them. People are hard-hearted around here.

I sit on the grass for twenty minutes waiting for Dad. The boys don't come out in that time, which is a shame because I sat on the ground to look pathetic and sad.

Dad's car pulls into the parking lot and I stagger stiffly to my feet, brushing wet grass off my butt. I get in the passenger seat.

"Daaaad."

He turns a worried face to me. "What?"

"I think I got *fired*."

He lights up with sympathy. "It sucks, doesn't it?"

"It sucks so much!"

"You feel really embarrassed but angry too."

"Right! I *know*. . . ."

"And the surprise, that makes it worse."

"Totally does."

We bond all the way home about being treated badly. We agree that we are the most unappreciated, brave people we know. We pull into the driveway. Dad turns off the car and sits, looking like he's thinking carefully about his next words.

"When you get *dumped* dumped," he says slowly, "it's even worse because they may well have seen you naked."

"That would be so much worse!"

"Yes, it is. If someone rejects you who has seen your butt, it's extra hurtful."

"I'm never going to take my clothes off in front of *anyone*," I say emphatically.

We get out of the car.

"Wait, Dad, was *that* the sex talk? It was a little brief."

"It was efficient! In ten seconds I turned one of my girls into a nun."

"Ha. Good luck with the other one."

chapter 15

You got dumped?! Weez, you're having real Boy Trouble now. Are you honestly never going to take your clothes off in front of anyone? I guess you won't have to buy matching underwear so there's a saving! Your mom said when she joined match.com she bought so much lingerie, they knew her by name in Victoria's Secret!

HANNAH! I have to wash my brain now!

Sorry. Forget I ever said that. How are your folks?

Good. Think I'll keep them. How are yours?

Ugh. If I find a receipt, I'm getting a refund. SO MUCH PRESSURE! If it wasn't for you and Candy Crush I'd chuck my phone and get some peace.

I trudge into school the next day feeling like I have *DUMPED* written on my forehead. Typical, Dad drops me off *just* as Roman and Gabe's mom does the same. Displaying the sort of perfect timing they can't achieve in a swimming pool, I think to myself and smirk meanly.

They don't say hi. No matter, they never did anyway. Gabe and I make eye contact and he gives me a fleeting smile. Between him and Melia, I've got two secret, silent "friends." My birthday party will be a riot.

I take my phone out—nothing. Hannah and I are talking a bit more, but nothing on WhatsApp. Dad's sent me a photo of his most recent job rejection. Dear Murk, it begins.

Only the coolest people get dumped, he writes underneath. Lots of love and best wishes, Murk Brown. (Do I sound like a paint color?)

As in, "We're going to paint the toilet Murk Brown"? I reply. Yes.

I sit by myself in physics—Operation: Make Friends is on hold for now. For once I don't mind having no one to talk to; I'm not in the mood to chat. I get out my physics book and doodle on it a list of reasons why it's for the best that I'm not working with the boys anymore.

1. I don't have to worry about being cool in front of them. (Hanging out with these boys is stressful—I always worry I'm about to reveal how lame my life is. E.g. when they talk about parties and I have nothing to contribute except the funny thing that happened when Mom and I went to the car wash. A dog walked through it and came out soapy. It was hilarious and I

97

tell it well, but it's a tragic insight into what I do on a Friday night.)

2. More free time? (Oh, whoopee.)

3. No more money. Hmm. More space in my wallet?

Once morning classes are done, I head off to the cafeteria. Standing in the line I notice that Melia is behind me, *and* without Cammie for once.

I decide to turn around and smile at her, and if she smiles back, I will upgrade this smile to a chat. Then from a chat we'll move toward eating lunch together. *Then* I'll just be a hop, skip, and a jump from a sleepover! And then we'll kick Cammie out of school and everyone will be happier without her. (*Cue music and balloons.*)

OK, better not get ahead of myself. First I have to trick Melia into chatting with me and enjoying my company. I swivel around and realize I'm too close, like I'm swooping in for a kiss.

I step back and open my mouth to say, "Hey!" or "How's it going?" or "What up, dawg?" (Probably not the last one.)

But she's looking down at her phone. I know she's seen me turn around for this brilliant chat we were about to mutually enjoy, but she's ignoring me.

I bet she's scared Cammie or Nicole or Amanda will see us talking and make fun of her. I *bet* that's it. I can even see her give a glance around the cafeteria for them. I bet they gave her a hard time for saying hi to me in the changing room the other day. Argh! Where do people get off being such mad control freaks?

Whatever. I'm going to have this chat whether she likes it or not; she can't ignore me. (She can ignore me. This could get extremely awkward.)

"How's it going?" I say.

"Cool."

"Great stuff. Bit of a line *again*."

"Yeah."

This is like milking a tortoise. No, blood from a stone, that's the saying.

"Any plans this weekend?"

"Not much."

I persevere but it's like she's holding up a big shield of Banter. She deflects my chat with things like "nightmare" and "great stuff" while I babble on, and everything she's saying means *nothing*. I get the distinct feeling she'd walk away if she weren't waiting for food.

"What can you do?" is the most I manage to get out of her before she goes back to looking at her phone. I stare at the top of her head for a few minutes, then get distracted by something *awful* happening on the other side of the cafeteria.

Roman is talking to Cammie. Not flirting, actually talking. She's nodding and he's gesturing at Gabriel, who's standing back like he doesn't want to get involved, and I just *know* he's asking if she or someone else on the team will coach them.

I feel so angry and jealous. Before I know what I'm doing, I leave the line and I'm striding toward them. Gabe looks up as I approach, and the surprise on his face brings me back to my senses before I march over there and bounce Roman's and Cammie's stupid, pretty heads together.

So what I actually do is blush bright red, march toward the most popular people in my school looking like a radish-faced killer, then at the last minute skip around them and run out of the cafeteria.

99

Even before the doors swing closed, I can hear a sudden gale of surprised laughter.

"What was *that*?!" a boy hoots, and I march down the corridor with no idea where I'm going, I'm just embarrassed and I want to be by myself.

Back in the library. My old plan B. Except this time I don't even have a sandwich to hide in my book.

My book.

I get out my big notebook and I stare at the routine again. With hindsight, it does look like it should be called A Fancy Way to Drown. But that's OK, because I suddenly realize that I have a secret weapon.

I WhatsApp the boys:

> Meet me at the pool at 7 tomorrow. If you don't feel we've made progress by the time we leave I'll give you last week's £20 back.

I stare at it before pressing Send. It's missing something. I move the cursor to the front of the message and add:

> I'm sorry. You are good swimmers. For boys.

The ticks appear, so I know it's been sent. I wait half an hour, then head back to class. All through my afternoon classes I keep checking my phone, but no one replies. In desperation, at four thirty I type:

Those girls can't coach you, they're
the competition! Plus do you really want
to flip upside down and choke on your
own snot in front of girls you like?

Bulletproof logic, and they seem to agree.

Gabriel
I'm in! It's good to nearly drown,
makes you appreciate life ☺
Roman
Go on then.
Pete
Same.

chapter 16

can't wait for the next day to pass so I can show the boys the new routine. So of course, every minute, every second, *draaaaags*. Mr. Peters calls me up to his desk after a double block of English, which I spent scribbling sneakily in my notebook.

"Lou," he says. "I promise, lessons don't drag when you pay attention. I was talking about *Hamlet*, one of the greatest stories in the world. And you were staring at a tree."

"I'm sorry," I say. He has a way of scolding that makes me feel so guilty. *This* is the sort of emotional blackmail I was trying on Debs and the boys, but I haven't got Mr. Peters's gifts.

He nods at Hannah's empty chair. "Are you missing Banquo's ghost?" he asks.

"I know why that's supposed to be funny," I tell him kindly.

"You could've laughed!"

"LOL."

"Go away, Louise. And stop killing time, *participate!*"

If only he could see me now, I think, as I set up a flip chart at the swimming pool that evening and set my big notebook on top. Totes participating.

I arrange my big fat marker pens at the bottom and wait for the boys. They arrive a minute later and all stand in front of my notebook. Finally Roman states the obvious.

"It's blank."

"Yes," I say. "I want you to tell me what you like doing and what you're good at, and then I will build a routine that you will enjoy. A routine just for *you*, to complement all your skills. And—sorry, that's what I should've said the other day. Not—"

"'I thought you were better swimmers!'" the three of them echo back at me. Oops, think I possibly hurt their feelings with that. I hold my hands up in a "Sorry" gesture. But it worked; they're already softening. They reach for pens and start doodling.

"And!" I say, pulling off my sweater, with my swimsuit underneath. "Let me give you some ideas."

I dive in from the side and start showing them barrel dives down to the bottom of the pool, and some shapes I can form while I'm down there. When I surface, Pete is shaking his head.

"I can't hold my breath that long!"

I bite back something I want to say but don't dare.

"You could if you quit smoking," Roman tells him sternly.

Bingo. That's the one.

I get them to hop in the pool and try out some easy exercises, and see if we can combine some to make them a little harder.

"Is there something we could do that lets us catch our breath between dives, something on the surface? Surface work? If that's a 'Thing'?" Gabe asks.

We all shrug at each other. Sure, "surface work," that sounds plausible.

I pretend to think as I pace casually over to my bag and peek at something hidden inside. It's *Swimming for Women and the Infirm*.

Surprisingly helpful if you're trying to teach yourself synchronized swimming and Wikipedia doesn't offer much. But if the boys knew, it would hurt their pride, so *shhh*.

The session goes so well, we even walk out together as four! It's like we're friends. (If you glance at us quickly, from a distance.)

"So should I work on the routine and we'll meet in two or three days?" I ask slyly.

"OK, then," says Roman. "And thanks."

"Really, thanks," adds Gabe. I planned parts of the routine to be easier on him. I don't want to exhaust him, and I think he knows that.

Pete holds out his hand. "The twenty quid?" he asks.

I look up, shocked. Is he joking? No, he's deadly serious. I think! The moment hangs in the air and I'm so confused. Then Roman slaps him on the shoulder, laughing, and the three of them walk off to Pete's car.

Oh, ha ha.

Gabe twists back to give me a little wave and an apologetic look. Pete's nice, deep down, but there are a lot of layers of rude knob-head to chisel away first.

Dad picks me up. I feel guilty now that I'm not fired anymore, but he doesn't feel like I've abandoned him.

"My employed daughter," he says, ruffling my hair, "is going to buy me fries."

"No!"

"Daddy's so proud!"

"*Small* fries. And no burger!"

chapter 17

Weez! Where are you?! I'm fed-up.
My times aren't getting any faster.

Sorry! I'm here I'm here. You're just plateauing,
Debs taught us that, it happens.

I've cut out carbs, yet every time they weigh us I get heavier.

You probably weigh more because you're gaining muscle.

Yeah, muscle on my fat butt and gut.

SHUT UP, FATTY.
Han?

all too soon it's the weekend again. This week has been OK—
Mr. Peters and I have agreed that I will participate in class and

he will never make a Shakespeare joke again. He said he had a brilliant one about Bottom, but I was adamant.

So classes are all right. Actually, they are definitely more interesting than staring out the window. And we've had two swimming training sessions, so it's almost like I have a Thing again! Although it's not my Thing, it's the boys' thing—I'm just helping them. Still, they need me (and my trusty copy of *Swimming for Women and the Infirm*).

I'm stuck in the house on Saturday morning, as usual. Lav is getting ready to go into town. I'm lying on my bed, watching her. I wish I had someone to go shopping with. I could ask Lav and she might take me with her, but her friends won't like it and I'll feel in the way.

I've already cleaned both cars and my half of the bedroom. Mom and Dad were watching me fearfully as I did this. They kept yelling, "What have you done? Why are you sucking up? Have you killed someone?!"

It was a relief when I finally put down the vacuum and said please could I go to the tryouts for *Britain's Hidden Talent*. It's in the daytime, three weeks from today, with two boys from school (and one boy who has left school and is in college and smokes . . . I *don't* say). Yes, of course we'll have an adult with us, Pete's dad.

No, I'm not dating any of the boys, good grief. Lav backed me up on this. They have nothing to worry about with me there.

"*Yet*," said Dad supportively.

Uh-huh. I'm sure I'll be inundated with boys chatting me up, aaaaany day now. I rolled my eyes, but I know he was just being nice.

They agreed I could go, as long as I promised to take my phone with me. (Like I'd leave it behind! I might miss Hannah telling me the calorie count of a peanut.)

My phone vibrates now. Probably another demand from Pete that I change the choreography of the swimming routine so it doesn't mess up his hair. (I'm not even joking.)

It's a WhatsApp message from Gabe saying that he just realized they'll need some matching swimming gear for the tryouts next week and is there any chance that I'm free today to go to the mall and find some?

There is a big, fat, wobbly chance I'm free!

I reply immediately: Love to, great idea!

Pete and Roman both reply saying they're busy—of course they are—but I don't care, because they make me nervous anyway. I'll have a much nicer time hanging out with Gabe.

"MOOOOM! Can I have a lift into town, please?"

"Your dad *just* took Laverne to the mall!"

I go to the top of the stairs. She's standing at the bottom, looking irritable.

"I'm sorry, I only just got asked."

Her eyes narrow. Mom-radar.

"By a *boy*?"

"Yes, but I swear not like that, Mom!"

"Oh, really?" She pulls a coat on and grabs her car keys. I take that as a yes and run downstairs.

"Wait, should I get changed?" I'm just in jeans and a T-shirt.

"If you get changed I'll know it is *like that*."

Fine. I won't get changed. I follow her out to the car, reassuring her of the nonromantic nature of my trip.

"Seriously, Mom, I could fit him in my pocket."

"He'll grow."

"So will I!"

We pass Dad driving back from dropping Lav off. Mom points at me with her thumb and gives him an exaggerated eye roll. I grab the steering wheel so we don't plow into a line of parked cars. Dad's laughing as he drives off.

I wait for Gabe outside the entrance to the shopping mall. I hope we have enough to talk about. We usually talk easily, maybe because he's the only one who's not scared that I like him. (For the record, I don't like Roman and Pete, but I feel like I *should*, and that makes me feel like they think I *do* and . . . oh shut up, it's complicated being me.)

But I only know Gabe through swimming training, not as someone I go shopping with. I hope it's not weird, like going to the zoo with your dentist.

I see him before he sees me. He's dressed in khakis and a denim shirt, which are either designer gear or he's so cool that everything looks designer on him. I tug at the hem of my old T-shirt self-consciously, realizing I probably smell of car-cleaning fluid. I'm such a sophisticated lady.

I have a sudden horrible thought—how do we say hello to each other? Kiss on both cheeks? That feels dangerously French. I picture a nightmare scenario where I grab Gabe firmly by his little shoulders and kiss him on both cheeks and he tells Pete and Roman that I'm a sex pervert. (I know that's not the right phrase.)

He's getting closer and I still haven't decided what to do. Argh! He's right in front of me!

"Hi," he says, and gives me a quick, friendly hug.

I'm an idiot. I follow him into a cheap sports shop.

"Will Roman and Pete wear something from here?"

"We'll cut the labels out and tell them it's Armani."

We go from shop to shop, trying to find something not too expensive but not cheap, not too baggy but not too clingy. (I blush so hard when Gabe holds up some tiny Speedos that I swear I feel the blood leave my feet.)

There's like a foot height difference between us—the wrong way, obviously—so I know we must look strange together, but I genuinely don't care. Until we walk past a big group of kids from Laverne and Gabe's year. They start laughing.

"Hey, Gabe, is that your girlfriend?" one guy yells. It's like he's being nasty to me but friendly with Gabe. My heart starts beating hard.

"My wife, actually, show some respect," Gabe replies coolly.

There's a confused silence from the group.

"She's massive!" another one calls out, and I look to Gabe, wondering how he'll handle this.

"I think the word you're scrabbling for is *statuesque*." He smiles back at them like he literally could not care less. And I guess he doesn't, so I don't either. As we walk away, I feel slightly shell-shocked. Judging from the silence behind us, I'm not the only one.

After an hour of intensive swimwear shopping, I've touched so much Lycra that my hair is all static and I keep giving Gabe electric shocks (like a feeble X-Man). We decide to get coffee and let the electrons dissipate.

We talk about school. I skim over my social status, but . . .

"That's what I'd heard about you," he says, spooning a mountain of sugar onto his coffee froth with a serious look on his face. It's very sweet.

His face, not the coffee, although probably both.

"What had you heard about me?" I'm astounded that he'd heard anything about me.

"You don't try to be like everyone else." He shrugs, like it's obvious. "You're not bothered about being popular or dressing cool or having boys like you."

It's a compliment; it just *really* doesn't sound like one. I let it pass.

"Who are *your* friends?" I ask, suddenly realizing I don't know much about him.

"People online, with similar illnesses. When I was out of school, we'd talk all the time. It's odd being back with people whose biggest problem is growing out bad bangs."

"Um, your illness. What exactly . . . ?" I trail off, wondering if I'm being nosy.

"It comes and goes," he says. "At its worst it's like having flu *all* the time. You're too exhausted to get out of bed, but you can't sleep and your limbs ache and you can't concentrate on anything. So it's like one long sleepless night."

"Wow."

"It's OK, really."

"Is it?"

"No. I'm just being totally brave and cool about it." He flips his hair back like Roman.

I laugh. And I can see that gang from his year watching us, which makes me laugh even harder. They must be shocked by the sudden improvement in my life. I know I am.

111

I stop laughing and we sit for a bit in a comfortable silence. Which goes on a little *too* long and suddenly becomes awkward. Argh! This Making New Friends is a minefield—you can't ever relax. I panic and say whatever comes into my head.

"And is there more of you?"

"You mean . . . ?"

"Sorry. I *mean*, do you have any other siblings?"

"No, just Roman." Gabe smiles as I wave my teaspoon around trying to finish this garbled question. I flick some milk froth over his shoulder.

"Sorry!"

"That's OK. And you have a sister, don't you?"

"Yeah, she's in your grade. Laverne Brown. Dark hair, big eyes. Really, you don't know her? *All* the boys in our school know who she is."

He's still shaking his head.

"She's nice. A little like your brother." I think about Lav rubbing oil into my hair, and I feel bad. "No, that's not fair. She's nicer than Roman."

There's a silence. I suddenly realize how rude that is.

"Not that Roman isn't nice, he's just . . ." I'm waving my teaspoon again. Gabe holds his napkin up to shield himself from any more flicked froth, and I smile and put the spoon down.

Wow, coffee really brings out the truth bombs.

"Perhaps," says Gabe, choosing his words carefully, "he feels like he can't be so good-looking and talented for no reason. His life feels smaller than he deserves."

"Poor guy," I say fake-seriously.

"And Pete's always been grumpy."

"But you're not."

"I'm just happy to be out of my pajamas."

"Congratulations," I say, and we cheers coffee cups. "Now that you are, let's get you into some Lycra."

That sounds sassy in my head, but once I say it . . . weirdly sexual.

We sit in silence with my strange, accidental flirting hanging in the air.

chapter 18

Louise.

I've told this you so many times that I'm worried you have brain damage. But once again: STAY OUT OF MY HALF OF THE ROOM. I'm trying to live like a dignified human being over here and you are a slob. It's bad enough that I have to look at it, but don't let it spill over into my half. Anything of yours that I find on my side of the room I'll throw out of the window.

Laverne.

No kisses.

Lav.

WHY ARE YOU EMAILING ME, I AM THREE FEET AWAY FROM YOU?!

I just watched you type that and you just watched me read it. Maybe you couldn't see me properly over the one sock, one notepad, and a pencil that's ALL OVER the floor. Aargh, the chaos!!

It's cool if you're on your period, but you don't have to advertise it.

Lou.

No kisses.

She is right: My side of the room is a state. It looks like Sports Direct exploded. (God forbid it ever does; that's where I get *all* my clothes.)

For the past three weeks, I've spent every lunchtime and evening with the boys, trying to do as much homework as I could in between classes, coming home, swallowing dinner, racing out to coach them, then coming back home and falling into bed. I am tired.com/pooped.

You know when you walk into a room and you can't remember what you went in there for? I did that today, in the bathroom.

The night before the tryouts, we have our usual training session. I've never seen the boys so nervous. Afterward we stand around the pool, talking through the routine one more time. We only stop when I get a very stern text from my dad telling me he's been sitting in the parking lot for half an hour and if I don't come out he's going to come in and get me.

I am wearing my shorts pajamas with the very short shorts, his message ends.

Terrified, I run to the car.

Dad says I'm too late for dinner so I'll have to go to bed hungry. I don't believe him for a second, and we get home to a lasagna in the oven. I hope he never moves out. Though I don't know how Mom would feel about that. Surely *one* day she'll have a successful date and end up with a boyfriend?

Heading up to bed full of anxiety and pasta, I get a sudden urge to tell Hannah how I'm feeling, but every time we talk lately she's just stressing about her training and her fitness and doesn't seem interested in me, so *fine*.

Her last text was about how all the other girls at the camp have a thigh gap, and do I have one?

> Yes, if I stick my butt
> out like a constipated duck.

I'd give my right leg for a thigh gap.

> If you lose a leg, you'll have
> all the thigh gap you want!

No reply.

the morning of the tryouts dawns bright and clear. Possibly. I wouldn't know. I don't wake up at dawn—I'm not a farmer.

My alarm goes off at five a.m., which is still *horrendous*, and Lav has a slurring, half-asleep tantrum at me.

I try to get ready without waking anyone else up, but the ancient plumbing in our house has other ideas. By the time it's belched out my hot water for a shower and flushed the toilet with a load of grumbling complaints, everyone is up. They're all staggering and yawning, bumping into each other, and getting tangled in their bathrobes. No one in this family functions well in the morning.

I sit at the bottom of the stairs waiting for the boys to arrive. Pete said his dad would come by in the pickup truck at 5:15 a.m. and can

I *please* stop questioning him about how he's getting the tank to the studio.

"NO!" I shout back to Mom. "I am *not* eating my packed lunch already!" Jeez, some people.

Oooh, cheese and pickle.

Lav comes and sits two steps behind me.

"Y'ellooo?" I greet her through a mouthful of cheese

"Are you going like that?" she asks.

"Lav, I'm about to line up in the rain for a million hours, then assemble a . . . sort of tank. I don't think it's a dressy day."

"No, that's what I *meeaan!*" She jumps up again and heads upstairs. "Haven't you ever lined up for a gig?" she yells over her shoulder. She comes back with a sleeping bag in her arms and piles of sweaters. "You will freeze your butt off," she informs me. "Then you will bore it off."

"So either way," I conclude, "I'm coming home without my butt. The one bit of my body that looks vaguely normal. That's a real shame."

I take the sleeping bag from her and start putting one of the sweaters on, when there's a terrifyingly loud hoot from outside.

Lav and I freeze. You know when you hear a dog and can just tell from its bark that it's a monster? Lav opens the front door and we peer out. There, blocking the whole road, is the biggest truck I've ever seen in my (admittedly not truck-filled) life.

It looks like the sort of thing you'd use to move a circus. Pete, Roman, Gabe, and a man in a baseball cap are all sitting in the front. Gabe gives me a queenly wave out of the window. The man in the baseball cap looks like he's tempted to stick him in the back with the tank.

"So. I guess that's my ride," I say.

"Please be careful!" Mom calls down from where she's peering out an upstairs window.

As if I *have* control over anything that happens today. I shoulder my sleeping bag and stagger out of the front door.

Our neighbors are starting to open their front doors to stare at this monstrosity in their road. I give them all a little wave, feeling like a celebrity.

The truck door opens three feet above my head and I look up at it helplessly. I've never had to jump *up* into a vehicle before. I guess this is how short people live.

Gabe reaches down for my stuff and then Roman reaches past him, makes a long arm, and pulls me up into the cab, where the boys are already squashed together. I land on the springy seat. It smells like an ashtray in here, and as Pete's dad nods at me, then taps his cigarette delicately onto the floor, I see how he's arrived at this smell.

"Hello, Mr. . . . ." I say. Then realize I don't actually know Pete's last name, so it sounds like I just called his dad "mister."

He grips his cigarette between his teeth and simply says, "Pete," while throwing the megatruck into reverse.

Pete's dad is called *Pete*?

Who gives their kid their own name and doesn't think that might get confusing when yelled around the house? You only give your child the same name as you if you're royalty or you don't plan on living with them.

Like I can talk. My parents are divorced, and you know the saying: People in glass houses . . . go to slightly smaller glass houses every other weekend to see their dad.

I sit back gingerly. The seat is sticky, but it's probably for the best, as there are no seat belts. Gabe and I make Big Eyes at each other, half "This is fun!" and half "Maybe today we'll die!"

Pete's dad slams on the brakes and we all lurch forward. Then he accelerates for about three fast inches and slams on the brakes again before going into reverse. We do this maybe ten times, and it gets nauseating pretty quickly.

My family has congregated at the front door, and I wave at them with a big smile on my face. I might as well. If this is the last time they ever see me, let's give them a happy memory. Gabe peeks around me and joins in. Mom makes a face like a ventrilo-quist's dummy and says something out of the corner of her mouth to Lav.

"He's nice-looking."

Lav makes the same face. "Short, though."

Dad weighs in with "growth spurt" mouthed nice and clearly. *Thanks, family!* I was just thinking, Heeey, it's almost six a.m. and my ears haven't burnt with shame once today.

Roman leans forward to give a friendly nod to my family. Then Pete's dad reverses into our neighbor's front yard and takes that pesky birdbath off their hands. Roman leans back out of sight.

Pete murmurs something in his ear.

"Oh, go on," I say. They turn to look at me.

"What?"

I sigh. "I know exactly what you're thinking. Just say it."

Roman says, "Your sister is gorgeous" at the exact same moment as Gabe says, "Your dad *does* have great legs for his age. . . . Oh wait, no, not that?" We all laugh, even Pete.

I feel a little bit bad laughing with my new friends *at* my family, but it's not mean and I secretly feel very happy.

Not friends. Did I say *friends*? I meant sports colleagues.

"Sooo . . ." I say, to fill the silence as we jerk backward and forward on our forty-one-point turn and I can see Dad wrestling with a breeze up his robe that threatens to shame us all.

"What's your surname, Pete?"

"Who's asking?" grunts his dad, fixing me with a stare. He couldn't be sketchier if he had a bag marked *Swag* over one shoulder. I can't believe he works at the aquarium. I wouldn't trust him with a fish finger.

"So, the tank, is it . . . ?" I wait for someone to leap in and finish my question, since I really don't know anything about fish tanks. But Roman and Gabe give me tiny shrugs—obviously they have no idea either—so I plow on alone. "Is it, like, ready to assemble, or . . . ?"

Pete's dad stares at me as if I've said something stupid, but I'm cool with not knowing anything about fish tanks. He chews his soggy cigarette over to the corner of his mouth and says, "I dismantled it to get it out the window. Gotta assemble it at the other end."

Get it out the window? I concentrate on breathing in through my nose and out through my mouth and try not to get stressed. While I'm doing that, Pete's dad picks up a screwdriver and hands it to me.

It's a sort of friendly gesture, like, "You and me, pal, can build this huge criminal tank."

Gabriel leans over and we scrutinize it together with exaggerated care, as if it's a dug-up dinosaur bone. I'm about to get the giggles so we stop. Pete's dad seems a bit unpredictable. Let's not poke the beast.

Driving in the megatruck is *so* exciting! We're kings of the road! (Kings in the old-fashioned sense where you slaughter people left, right, and center.) Roman, Pete, Gabe, and I spend most of the journey ducking down to look in the sideview mirrors, praying that each cyclist we drove past is still upright and moving. Thankfully, they all are. I don't think I've ever seen so many rude gestures before in my life.

I'm wishing someone from school could see me with the guys, but—just my luck—we're too high up to be seen. Maybe I could take an "accidental" selfie . . .

chapter 19

Weezy, I'm so busy here, it's manic, I feel like I barely have time to think. I just swim swim swim and I'm always nervous! Mom's being crazy and I haven't so much as SEEN a carb in days. I miss them, and you. Do you miss me?

Miss you.

Hxxxxxxxx

I'm trying to text Han back, but the truck's bouncy suspension makes me feel sick. I'll tell her the good news when we get through the tryouts. Eventually the megatruck pulls up outside a massive modern building. It's got huge walls made of windows. Must be a nightmare to clean, I tut to myself, sounding like Dad.

There's a line of hundreds of people sheltering under umbrellas, and here we are, pulling up in the megatruck like total bosses. I have never felt cooler. I'm nearest to the window, so I roll it down and lean out supercasually, like I own the truck. Mmm hmm, yes, I look young for my age.

I've never seen the appeal in smoking, but right now I'd love to fling a cigarette out the window with a world-weary gesture like, "Hey, it's just another TV gig."

Pete Senior opens his window, flicks his soggy cigarette out with a world-weary gesture, and follows it with a gob of spit.

Less TV Star, more Loitering Outside Pawn Shop.

I eye the posters for upcoming gigs. I've never been to a gig here (or anywhere, if I'm honest), but Lav's been to a couple with her friends.

"Oh, I've been here," says Roman. "I came for a soccer sticker swap meet years ago. They made us line up outside in the rain for three hours."

"That's ridiculous!" I say.

"Nah, we only stayed forty minutes, did all our swaps in the line, and by the time they opened the doors, we'd gone."

"All right," wheezes Pete's dad, "let's park." He puts the hand-brake on and swings himself out of the cab. Really? Here?

We clamber down and join Pete's dad next to his "parking space." It looks as if we just parked in the middle of a square—you know, the sort of place where people eat sandwiches, drink a coffee with friends, and *don't* park trucks?

"You bunch go get in the line," says Pete's dad, wrestling with the doors at the back. "I'll unload."

"Should we help?" Roman asks Pete.

"Heavy work, lads," Pete Senior sniffs.

"Don't bother offering," Pete tells him, walking away. "When my dad looks at me, he just sees a seven-year-old in a tutu."

Pete did *ballet* as a kid? Roman sniggers. I don't think I was meant to hear that. I hang back so he doesn't realize I did.

"Shut up, Ro. You never heard of *Billy Elliot*?"

I want to join in, but I still don't feel like one of them, so I don't risk it.

At the front of the line is a massive opening into a huge warehouse-looking area. You could park a plane in there and then lose it when you came back from your shopping.

We peer in. It's full of cameras and men with walkie-talkies and young women with clipboards, and big black floor-to-ceiling curtains partitioning off different sections. I'm nervous at the thought of being in the middle of that madness. But that won't be for a while, because first we have to get in line.

The line is about five deep; the people at the front are sprawled on the floor as if part of a disastrous sleepover. They're giving off a nasty whiff—sports sock full of egg—and look crazy around the eyes.

We walk along the line, looking—hoping—for the end of it. We walk and we walk, and the line just keeps on . . . *being*. After we follow it around the building for over five minutes, it no longer looks like a queue; more like a medium-sized country with a whimsical sense of humor said, "Hey, guys, let's stand in a sausage shape today!"

There are a lot of dogs in dresses. This is going to be a day I'll never forget. (Which can be a good thing and a bad thing. I'll never forget the day I had chicken pox and got a scab up my nose.)

A ferret wearing a tiny cowboy hat darts at Gabe's ankle, teeth bared.

"Anastasia, no!"

Her owner, a skinny teenager with gauges in each ear, scolds her and scoops her up.

By now we're at the end of the line. I think Gabe would rather be farther away from the ferret.

"Who names a ferret Anastasia?" wonders Roman.

"The sort of person who dresses it up in a cowboy hat," Gabe says.

Pete looks worried. "I hope there are some normal people here, that we're not just auditioning for a freak show."

Now he worries about that?

"Underwater synchronized dancing probably fits right in," mutters Roman, who seems to be losing his nerve. I have to do something.

I give a little peep on my whistle and they all look at me.

"Let's sit and wait and stay focused," I tell them with a confidence I do not feel. Thankfully, no one argues back.

I pull on another sweater and wriggle into my sleeping bag. After a few minutes of squirming, I finally slide into a comfy position. I look up to find all the boys watching me.

"Have you never lined up for a gig?"

We sit there *forever*. OK, forty minutes, but that's a really long time to sit on the ground. The line keeps moving forward tiny bit by tiny bit, which is such a pain in the butt—literally—'cause I'm shuffling along on my bum every thirty seconds to keep up. Eventually the boys take pity on me and drag me behind them like a bag of garbage.

I will really need to wash my hair, I think as I feel it scrape along the tarmac.

More and more people join the line behind us, so at least we feel like we're ahead of *someone*. Just then I see a very unwelcome sight: an upside-down view of Debs, Cammie, Melia, Nicole, and Amanda walking past us. Cammie stops when she sees Pete. I sit up and knock a candy wrapper out of my hair.

Debs notices her team has stopped and comes back to see what's happening. "Oh, hello," she says, vaguely drifting her eyes over everyone as if she doesn't really remember us. Cheers, ex-favorite teacher. She recognizes the boys and I see her putting two and two together. So that's what we were doing at the pool.

"Are you going to line up?" I ask.

"No," she says. The girls smile a little, like, "Oh, how LOL, but I can't laugh or I'd crack my makeup."

"We got through weeks ago," says Debs smoothly. "We're here to do interviews, dress rehearsal with our bespoke swimming pool . . . you know."

I nod, but I don't know, especially the word *bespoke*.

I hope it means "full of snakes."

"Uh-huh," says Gabe. (Love Gabe, he's never rude to anyone. I'm so glad he's picked up on the tone here. The other two are just dribbling over the girls. Please focus, team.) "Yah, we've got a freestanding swimming pool too. Ours is industrial, though, higher build quality—well, you know . . ." he says, having an elaborate stretch and yawn to show how very unbothered he is.

I'm quietly Googling *bespoke* on my phone, inside my sleeping bag so Debs can't see. Oh, it just means someone made it for them. Well, someone's making our pool for us, *actually*, so . . .

"Hey!" comes a yell from behind. Great timing, Pete Senior.

"Heyy!!!" he says again, clearly feeling that the whole line should be listening. "I've got yer fish tank set up!"

chapter 20

At the words *fish tank*, I can see everyone in the line starting to giggle and look around. To be clear about this, these are people who put hats on their ferrets and dresses on their dogs, and they are laughing at *us*.

"Thanks, Dad!" yells Pete, leaping to his feet. Then he sees the tank and his face droops. I haul myself up using Gabe as a crutch, stumble over a few magazines, and shuffle to stand next to Pete. And we stare together.

Well. If one were to scrabble around for a nice thing to say (and let's be nice, why not?), it looks a bit like modern art. It lurches and bulges wonkily at the sides. I can't imagine it holding a small mouse, let alone gallons of water. And it's really small—the swimming routine is going to involve a lot more cuddling than I'd choreographed.

Also, *how* are we going to move it into the studio? Already a traffic cop is eyeing it and reaching for his notebook.

"I won't keep you," I say crisply to Debs and her team. They drift off with a couple of pitying backward glances and snickers.

"Stay here," says Pete wearily to me. "Hold our place." Happy to! His dad was tetchy when I asked him his surname; imagine how moody he'll get when questioned about his crazy fishbowl. I watch the three boys slope away from me and toward the wobbly upside-down greenhouse in the middle of the pedestrianized zone.

My stomach is churning with cheese, worry, and pickle. I fiddle with my whistle, which usually bolsters my confidence, but right now I feel out of my depth. I look at my phone and think about calling home, but I've got no bars.

Pete, Roman, and Gabe finish talking with Pete Senior and walk back to me with faces of men who have seen their own doom and know there is nothing left to do but face it with dignity.

"Good news?" I say brightly.

Gabe looks at Pete, who says nothing, so he fills me in. "We have no idea how we can move it from out here to in there. And that tank is so small, if we attempt the triple dive, someone's going to end up pregnant. And it can't be me, because I need to focus on my education."

I sink deep inside my sleeping bag. All this hard work for nothing! After a few seconds, I poke my head back out to see what's going on. They've fallen silent. Roman and Gabriel are staring at Pete in utter astonishment.

"What?" I demand, pushing my hair out of my face. "What have I missed?"

"Pete just apologized," whispers Roman.

"Do it again," says Gabriel incredulously.

"Oh, shut up!" snaps Pete. "I'm sorry, OK? I really thought my dad would come through for me."

"To be fair . . ." I say slowly.

"Oh, seriously, Lou, can you not?" interrupts Pete. How is *every-one* allowed to make fun of him except me?

"I wasn't going to!" I protest. "I was going to say that he got a gigantic truck across town, carrying a quite big and" (I hiss this bit) "*stolen* fish tank in it, *and* he managed to put it together, sort of. Your dad did all that because he loves you (and is criminally reckless), but it's still amazing." I trail off, suddenly becoming shy again.

Pete's dad ambles up.

"No good, then?"

We hesitate.

"It's brilliant, Dad, thanks," lies Pete, and hugs his dad, who gives him a surprisingly comfortable hug back.

"Thanks, Pete!" we all say with big fake smiles.

"Good," says his dad. "Call me when you need me. I'll be in the pub."

"Aaahh," says Gabe as we watch Pete Senior wander off. "I love to hear those words from the man who's driving me home in a ten-ton truck."

There's a shrieking, scratching noise behind us, and we turn around just in time to see the tank collapse in on itself. A raggedy cheer and a round of applause rises up from the line.

So it's come to this, I sigh to myself. Plan B—as in Bloody Stupid.

I wriggle out of my sleeping bag and divest myself of a couple of sweaters. I'm walking to my doom, and I don't want to look like a laundry basket that sprouted legs. I've been formulating a desperate idea for the past ten minutes that I really hoped I wouldn't have to put into action. I head toward the TV cameras at the front of the line.

I see Debs from the back; she's standing just inside the entrance to the aircraft hangar. She's leaning on one leg slightly, hand on hip. Even when she's relaxed, Debs always looks ready to pounce and kill. Which doesn't help right now.

"Debs?" I say. She doesn't turn around. She's watching her girls give an interview to two smooth-faced men holding microphones.

"COACH!" I yell, and she wheels around. Instinct.

"Can I talk to you?" I ask.

"Not now." She turns back, dismissing me. Hannah would do this so much better than me, but she's not here, so it's up to me. I grab hold of my inner Hannah and take a deep breath.

"Durbs!" I announce in a reedy shout. Oops, spit bubble in my throat.

Ahem.

"Debs!" I shout less froggily. "I'm sorry I didn't swim fast enough at the Olympic time trials. I'm sorry that after all your coaching and hard work, I just wasn't good enough! I'm a failure!" The camera hovers over to me.

"But now I've coached a team of swimmers for this show, and it's helping me feel confident again! I just want a chance to show what we can do and make my gran proud. My gran who . . . died." I shield my eyes so I don't cry (very little risk of that TBH—both my grans are fine). The crowd around me murmurs sympathetically. I've seen this show; I know how it works. I lift my face out of my hands and do Big Eyes at Debs.

"So please, Debs, can we borrow your—bespoke pool?" The world goes very quiet as I stare at her and wonder what she'll do next.

Debs has a peculiar look on her face and I realize she doesn't know what to *feel*, let alone fake. I really have got her on her weakest area here. Genius, Lou! And only a little bit humiliating for me, but no worse than having tampons flicked at your head.

"That's a beautiful story," says one of the presenters, putting an arm around each of us. From the look on Debs's face, I'd be surprised if he gets that back in one piece.

"Great backstory. I know we can't wait to see these two former Olympic teammates become rivals today." He's not really talking to us; he's twinkling at the camera. Debs looks homicidal, so I say, "Thanks, Coach!" and run off.

"Hey!" A man with a walkie-talkie gestures to me. I hesitate, bouncing on the balls of my feet. "The pool will be here. Come and find us when you're a hundred away from the head of the line, OK?" I nod and run off to tell the boys.

chapter 21

my team is so pleased with me that they spend a ten on snacks from the local gas station and shower me in chips. An hour later, the chips are all gone and my hair feels salty, but I feel happy. This audition might actually happen. I make the boys stretch so their muscles don't stiffen up. They protest that they look stupid.

I nod at a woman dressed as a cow. This is not the place for shy people. Now get stretchy.

Roman keeps running to the head of the line to count back and see how far away we are from the front. Finally he sprints back, shouting, "Ninety eight!"

"OK, people, this is go, go, go!" I say, sounding a bit like Debs. We sprint to the entrance. I'm blinking in the unfamiliar darkness when a blank-faced security man puts his hand on my chest.

"Sorry, sir . . ."

I take out my hair clip, and my hair tumbles down.

He takes his hand off my chest *very* quickly and begins

apologizing. I walk past him and find my walkie-talkie guy, who is standing on top of a big podium, shouting and pointing at things. Everyone's very busy here, in a sort of "Behold my busy-ness, marvel at my loud efficiency!" kinda way.

"Excuse me!" I shout up at him, my voice sounding all weedy in the aircraft hangar. I'm aware that the security guard will soon be hot on my heels.

"It's me, swimming-pool girl? Can we have a look at the pool we're borrowing, please?" He nods at me and whispers something stern to his wrist. I hope he's got a microphone up there; our last pool provider was a little mad; we need this one to be less so.

"OK," he says, stepping down from the podium and heading toward us. He's listening to something in his earpiece and talking to us but looking three feet above our heads.

"They're just finishing up in there. The girls were doing a demo for the cameras." He jerks his head toward a big black curtain behind him. I'm desperate to see Debs's routine, and I step forward without thinking. Wrists Man puts a hand up to stop me.

I can hear splashing and bare feet padding around in there, some murmured thank-yous, then silence. Wrists Man peers around the curtain and nods at us to go through, holding it open for us. Gabe plucks at my arm in excitement, I pluck his back, painfully hard, and we do "Eeee!" faces at each other. We step through the curtain and stop, dazzled by the bright studio lights.

The pool is a huge, freestanding circle, about twelve feet high. It dwarfs us, and it takes me a few seconds to walk all the way around it, running my fingers admiringly over its sides.

All the way around . . . its . . . sides.

The sides are made of black plastic. I can't see into the pool. Of course, because they're doing normal synchronized swimming. I'm an idiot.

I keep walking until I bump into the boys. Pete is resting his forehead on the side, looking suddenly very tired.

"You can't see in," he says, though there's no need. Gabe picks at one of the edges.

"It won't come off," he adds.

Roman thumps his head a few times against the side of the pool. Debs appears. "Stop that. It's bespoke."

We walk back outside in silence, past Wrists Man and the presenters, who look confused about the kids who skipped into the studio and trudged out minutes later, all hope gone. Once we're outside we turn left as if to rejoin the line when we realize there's no point.

"You didn't even *see* the pool?" Pete asks.

"No!" I say. "I couldn't, 'cause it was backstage and I didn't even think. I . . . I just thought I'd fixed everything," I trail off miserably.

"Never mind," says Roman, but he doesn't sound at all like he means it.

We head toward Pete's dad's truck, as it seems the only thing left to do. Mom calls as we walk. I answer and tell her what happened in a half whisper. Right now I feel like Pete and Roman are having to stop themselves from yelling at me. This isn't fair. I did my best. Gabe puts a comforting arm around my shoulders. (Luckily, I'm stooped with sadness, or he would have struggled to reach.)

Mom hangs up and, just as I'm thinking, Never mind, in a couple of hours I'll be in bed eating cheese on toast, I see that the mega-truck has been booted.

Then I see Pete Senior weaving toward us with the snooty air of a drunk person who's trying to hide it, and I'm grateful that it has. Dad does this at Christmas: "Ah am *shimply* overwhelmed by all the festivitivitivi . . . turkey."

"Oh, balls," says Pete Senior, and gives the boot a halfhearted kick. He takes it very well, I must say, but I guess if you don't plan ahead, you're less fussed when plans suddenly change.

We stand around the collapsed fish tank while Pete's dad makes a series of phone calls to friends. Not standing too close in case it collapses further and also because a bored line of hopeful *BHT* contestants are taking selfies in front of it. They're all blatantly going to end up online, and I don't want to be tagged.

Not that I'm on Facebook. It's one thing to not have *loads* of friends, but there's no need to flaunt it publicly.

Pete's dad fetches us coffee from the gas station. Mine tastes like licking a battery and is not going to help my stomachache, but I feel so adult. Finally three cars turn up, driven by men who all nod at Pete before having huddled chats with his dad. They each take a shard of glass and wedge it in the back of their car. It's quite impressive, like ants transporting a leaf.

A leaf that will slice your head off if you brake too suddenly. I'm glad we're not traveling with them.

Hang on—how *are* we getting home? We look at each other as the last car leaves and realize, yup, our TV dreams have gone so badly wrong that we arrived in a megatruck but we're leaving by bus. Hello, Hollywood!

135

Hollywood Bowl, just off the traffic circle, that's my stop.

We ride the bus in dejected silence. I'm WhatsApping Lav. As I type, something rubs against my chest. It's my whistle, tucked under my T-shirt. I hold it for comfort.

"OK," I say suddenly. "This wasn't our last chance. There is one more public tryout. It's next week, and we will be ready. We have one week to *find a tank*. We're ready, the routine is ready. We can do this."

The boys look doubtful, as do the people around us on the bus. So I pull out my whistle and give it a quiet but encouraging peep.

"We CAN!" I repeat.

"Yeah." Gabriel nods. "OK."

"Yeah," says Roman, starting to smile.

"Yes!" says a man sitting behind me, caught up in the mood of the moment. He is not joining the team.

After a pause, Pete shoots me his first smile since he saw Debs's *bespoke* pool.

One week—we can do this. I hold tight to my whistle. I am a coach and this is my team.

chapter 22

Lou

Oh god, Lav, DISASTER at *BHT*.

I don't know where to begin.

Lav

I've got the headlines.

Lou

How do you know already??

Lav

Twitter.

Lou

AAARRRGGH!!! **Kills self**

Lav

No no it's OK, it's not that bad I swear.

Lou

Really? HOW?!

Lav

Most people are misspelling your name.

Lou

. . . LOU?

Lav

People are idiots.

Lou

Are they misspelling Roman,
Gabe, or Pete?

Lav

No.

Lou

I feel awful.

Lav

This will all blow over. Remember
when that upperclassman wet herself
in assembly?

Lou

No.

Lav

Exactly.

No wonder Roman and Pete were so grumpy. They have cool to lose, unlike me. Still, I don't like the way they snapped at me when things went wrong. I was trying my best, and the whole thing is not my responsibility. I'm two years younger than them, and they treat me like their mom *and* a servant.

But I'm not going to get resentful about it. I've done enough feeling sorry for myself this summer. We just have to find a tank.

(However many times I say that, it still sounds ridiculous.)

That night I go to bed early, tired out after the five a.m. start and all the public humiliation. Thankfully, my parents didn't make me go through it all again when I got in. Dad just handed me a giant candy bar.

I lie in bed, feeling bizarrely optimistic despite everything. At least I'm not dealing with this alone.

I wish I could talk to Hannah about it. Lav isn't the same—she knows more than me, so it feels more like advice than conversation. Right on cue, she addresses me from the opposite bed. No "Are you awake?" or any of that polite nonsense. Lav has decided it's Chat O'clock, so Chat Hats on and off we go. She looks up from her phone, musing.

"The trouble with boys," she says seriously, "is that they will invariably try to kiss you."

I can't help it—I start laughing.

"Yes, Laverne," I reply, "that is my problem with boys. They are always trying to kiss me. I am like bread in a duck pond. Also I wish they would stop writing me love songs; it gets tedious."

There is a thoughtful silence.

"Are you being sarcastic?"

"*Yes*! Yes, of course I'm being sarcastic. Good *grief*, Laverne, look at me."

She snaps her bedside light on and stares at me. "You're so pretty," she says.

"Don't," I say firmly. "Even to be nice. I am *huge*. My hair is crazy. I am ripped with muscles. *I* would be scared to meet me down a dark alleyway."

"You're like one of those androgynous catwalk models!" she protests.

"That may be, but this is not a catwalk in Milan. This is a

suburban town where men yell out of cars to ask if I've escaped from a zoo."

"I'm going to give you a makeover," she says firmly.

I sigh. Laverne thinks that makeovers are the answer to all of humanity's problems. If you dropped her into a war zone, she'd start shaping everyone's eyebrows.

I feel my eyebrows. They are pretty bad, actually, like slugs covered in dog hair. I try to comb them with my fingernails into roughly the right direction.

"Just leave it, Lav," I say quietly into the darkness. I say I don't care, but I guess I do, because I feel my throat grow hot and tight.

"Come here," she says, leaping out of bed and grabbing me by the arm. It is *so* scary when someone light-footed does that in the dark. She leads me out of our room, and we feel our way along the hallway to Mom's room, where she's trying to sleep.

"Mom," says Lav, "isn't Lou pretty?" Mom pushes her eye mask up and stares at us groggily.

"She's going to be," she answers.

"When?" I demand.

"Soon."

Uh-huh. I'd like a more specific time frame on that, TBH. I don't want to die just before I get pretty, with everyone at my funeral saying, "Such a shame. She finally grew into that nose."

Lav flops down next to Mom and I crawl in the other side. Mom groans but throws the duvet over both of us.

"You're too big for this," she tuts.

"Mom, don't fat-shame."

"Shut up, Laverne," she mumbles.

We lie still for a bit.

"Mom?" I whisper.

"Yes," she whispers back.

"Is Dad OK?"

I know Lav isn't asleep. She's listening too.

"He will be."

"Are you guys going to get back together?"

"No, he'll find a pretty redhead and they'll have lots of little sheds together."

"Mom."

"Go to sleep."

chapter 23

8:30
Great performance yesterday, guys, not a single weak link.
This is the strongest team I've ever coached. A few of you will
be following Hannah soon.

Debs

8:31
Thanks, Debs!

Nic x

8:33
Thanks, Debs! BTW, Lou is still on this group thread, can we
take her off it? ☺

Cammie xxxxx

apparently, creativity works best within constraints—I read that
somewhere. I have to remind myself of this on Monday when we

find that Debs has booked the swimming pool every evening this week, and we have nowhere to practice. I knew she'd do something like this. She's making sure we're not ready for the next tryouts.

The boys don't always manage the final lift where Gabe is raised out of the water, Pete and Roman each holding a foot. He balances there, leaning forward in a controlled lean, before the boys throw him up into a high graceful somersault.

Half the time they perform this perfectly; the rest of the time they slap him into the pool with a loud belly flop. Gabe says not to worry, he never wanted kids anyway.

I got that joke ages after he made it.

My little emotional blackmail trick at the tryouts has backfired, and Debs is now watching me like a hawk in hot pants. The situation is so desperate that Ro actually *talks to me in public*. Alert the media.

We're standing next to the vending machine at break time, and he stares intently at the chocolate throughout the conversation so no one will think he's talking to the big muscly weirdo two grades below.

"I don't know where else we can go. I'm sorry!" I tell him for the thousandth time.

"Well, *think*," he says impatiently. "This is your job."

"No, *actually*," I tell him, "my job was helping you put together an underwater routine without you all drowning. I have done that, and I have worked SO hard on this . . . so . . . don't tread on me."

You go, girl! I'm glad I had the guts to say that. Pete and Roman can get so focused on what *they* want that they don't care about anything or anyone else.

If only you could put Gabe's sensitive head on top of one of their bodies. Mmmm Frankenstein boyfriend.

I get a WhatsApp from Pete in math, where for once I'm enjoying being left alone in my own seat. Our math teacher *loves* making us pair off to do math exercises together. Why? When do you ever do math as a little double act? Pairing off doesn't make math more fun, like we're good cop, bad cop! We're mavericks, but we get results!

All that happens is that no one wants to be my partner, so I have to pair up with the teacher. Who doesn't help me, because *she is the math teacher and knows the answers.*

The WhatsApp says: *Outside the pool at 9 tonight. Wear dark clothes.*

Srsly? If Mom knew a boy had sent me such a sketchy text, we'd be straight down to the police station! Although the thought of Roman—or Pete—thinking of me That Way is hilaire. I'm not sure either of them *realizes* I'm a girl. I message back:

> I'll bring weapons, you sort alibis.

Roman
Cool
Pete
K
Gabriel
Oh man I am NOT going back to prison.

Two people in this team are really doing all the heavy lifting funny-wise.

I'm just putting my phone back in my pocket when it buzzes with a new email from Hannah. I skim-read with one eye on the teacher. Hannah's starting to worry me; she sounds more and more stressed. I hope her parents aren't giving her a hard time, or that the camp isn't picking up where they leave off. The last thing she needs is to be tag-teamed.

"Lou—eeze!" snaps Ms. Kearney.

"Four!" I call out. (Yell a number—it's always worth a try.) But from the look on her face, it was wrong. And from the silence in the room, it was quite funny. If I say something embarrassing, it's like someone's detonated an LOL bomb in the classroom, but funny gets nothing.

Lav is so right. They're not friends I haven't made yet; it's just bad luck they were born near me. I moodily doodle a fish tank on my math book. I put Cammie in it, add a shark, and leave them to it.

chapter 24

Weez are you there? I've had such a bad day. My times have
started getting worse, I feel really sluggish. I'm homesick too
and eating to feel better, but that's the LAST thing I should do.
Told Mom I want to come home, she said she won't let me
make a mistake I'll regret. So I'm stuck here. Come bust me
out?! Joking not joking.

Hx

that evening I eat dinner thinking about Hannah and whether I
should talk to my parents about her. Or maybe Lav or Mr. Peters?
Debs? No way, not Debs, mad idea.

I feel like showing her emails to anyone would be disloyal. I
reply and tell her to stay calm, that she's probably just having an off
week (or month . . . I don't add). I send her some photos of us camping and a few badly stuffed animals. If they don't make her smile.
then she's in real trouble.

It's only when the clock strikes seven that I remember I have a more immediate problem. I haven't asked Mom and Dad for permission to go out tonight. How can I? *Moooom, Daaaad, can I go out late at night with three boys you don't know? Uh huh, yes, I also suspect we're off to do something iffy. Don't wait up! And has anyone got money for vodka?*

It's time to call in some favors. I corner Lav as we're washing up after dinner, and I tell her the problem.

"Wow." She pauses midscrub. "That almost sounds cool. Who are you and what have you done with Lou?"

"Ha ha," I say. "But, help me. You've sneaked out loads of times to meet boys. How do you do it?"

"Not 'loads of times'!" she protests.

"Lav, I used to see you *walk past* my window on the flat roof. I didn't think Santa Claus had lost weight."

"Ah, was that when we had our own bedrooms?"

"Oh yes. The glory days. Over now."

"You tell them you feel ill and need to go to bed. You say your tummy and back hurt. . . ." She winks at me.

I wink back.

She winks again.

"Lav, why are we winking?"

"Oh, for goodness' sake. If I have to spell it out . . . When's your period due?"

"Er . . . the futuuure?"

"Seriously, you haven't started?"

"I'm all muscle-y, and my BMI is a little . . . and shut up, OK? Don't make me self-conscious about it!"

"I just thought you were dealing with it without any fuss."

"Oh no, when it happens, I will make fuss. Now go back to the winking."

"OK, when you say your tummy and back hurt, Dad hears period alarm bells and he'll give you a hot-water bottle and leave you alone."

"Brilliant!"

"Yes, *but* Mom will become *more* interested in you and hover around. There's a book called *Blossoming into a Woman* that is literally the worst book ever written, and she'll want to read it with you. However, she's going out tonight, so the plan is solid."

"What time is she heading out?"

"Eight forty-five."

"I've got to meet them at nine."

"So you're blossoming at eight forty-six, sharp."

It's now 8:50 and Mom *still* hasn't gone out. She's sitting on the sofa all dressed up, but she seems pretty happy watching TV with Dad. They're shouting insults at the news and laughing 'til they snort.

Lav and I sit stony-faced watching them. Every time they glance in our direction, we slap big smiles on our faces like, "Good one! David Cameron, huh?" (No idea. I have too many problems in my life to care about national ones.) *Finally* at nine, Mom kisses all of us and heads out—to meet Dan, whoever he is. Apparently, he's "in stocks." Makes me think of a medieval man with his head in stocks being pelted with rotten veggies. Best of luck, Mom.

The moment the front door slams, I look at Lav. She shakes her head. We wait, and there's the familiar sound of Mom's car starting up and driving off.

Lav nods. Operation: Blossom is a go.

"Ooh" I say, "my stomach hurts."

"Oh dear," says Dad, eyes on the TV.

"And my back," I add. "And I feel sort of emotional."

Lav shoots me daggers. Too much.

Dad gives me his full attention now. "Would you like a hot-water bottle?"

"I'll get it," Lav says, giving him a Look. "Maybe Lou should have an early night."

"OK," I say, like, "if you think I should."

"Feel better, Goldfish!" Dad calls as we shuffle upstairs slowly.

"That was awful, just in case you were wondering," Lav hisses, poking me in the back as she follows me up.

"Sorry, Lav, I've never rebelled before."

We change pace the moment we reach the bedroom. It's 9:03, and it takes me ten minutes at least to run to the swimming pool. *Argh!*

I shake off my bathrobe, and underneath I'm dressed like a mime. Head-to-toe black. Quite a nice outfit, actually, as Lav supplied most of it.

I put one foot out the window, ready to drop gently onto the flat roof and sneak off over the garage and down via the rainwater barrel, as instructed. And *not* snag the clothes on anything. Crucial instruction. Lav says if I rip her clothes, I should keep running, never look back, and live life on the run. It's a bit tempting, given how much I hate school.

I turn back and Lav is expertly folding clothes and pillows to stuff under the duvet. She glances up at me.

"Just in case he comes up. I'll stay here now and tell him you are asleep. Now hurry, you're late. Go make a cool evening uncool."

I drop gently onto the roof and run like a cartoon burglar over the garage with pointed toes and fingers. Hee hee, this is *fun*! When I get to the edge, I sit down and hook my legs over the side, feeling for the garbage can with one foot. I have to be careful; the top is slimy with mildew. I reach downward, further and further, but still can't feel it. I've got like the longest legs of anyone I know. How are they letting me down now?

I decide to drop the last couple of inches.

I let go and fall eight feet to the ground, hard.

I land on the balls of my feet, then fall backward onto my butt and elbows: classic gymnast's dismount. So *where* was the garbage can? I stand up quickly and bash my shoulder against it. Oh, there it is, a quarter of an inch to the left. Great work, Lou. That's going to bruise.

I'm really late now, but as I step forward, I crash into something big and confusing. It's metallic, with loads of sticky-out bits that hit me in the stomach, legs, and face, and I lose my balance and fall on top of it.

I fight it for a while; it seems to be covered in moving parts. Is Dad building a *torture machine* out in the middle of the yard?

I can't believe it—he's usually so fussy about putting things away. And not a psychopath.

I finally fight off the Machine of Pain, adding a few more bruises to the collection. It's been a pretty unstealthy few minutes, and I can picture Lav standing at the bedroom window, shaking her head and wincing at every crash as her idiot sister pratfalls over everything she can find.

I stand and wait for my eyes to adjust to the darkness. It was an upside down bike. Of course it was. Something else that Dad's "repairing." Once I can see better, I feel my way out of the side gate and start running.

I'm a fast runner, and without a bag full of books I make great time sprinting along the road. As I approach the pool, I can just about make out the three boys loitering in the gloom, impatiently pacing around the parking lot. Pete's fiddling with a cigarette packet but not smoking.

I bound up to them and they all jump about six feet.

"What are you doing?" Roman snaps.

"Did I fwighten you?" I snigger before shyness stops me. Surprisingly, Pete laughs.

"I'm sorry!" I tell them all. "I couldn't get away sooner! I had to wait for my mom to leave and then fake a . . . an illness for my dad."

"Why?" asks Roman, baffled.

I stare at him. "Why? Because I'm fifteen."

Gabe laughs. "She can't just stroll out the house like, 'Don't wait up, guys, I'm taking the car!'"

"You're fifteen?" say Roman incredulously.

"Yeah?"

"You look *much* older," he says, in a way that doesn't feel like a compliment. But fine.

"Right," Pete says, bored of this chitchat and snapping on a professional-looking flashlight. "Follow me."

We walk past the swimming pool and through one of the school fields, which is just behind it. It's seriously creepy. I wouldn't do this alone, but Roman and Pete lead, with me and Gabe following. Roman doesn't seem to be able to let the age thing go.

"Did you know she was only fifteen?" he asks Gabriel.

"Yes," says Gabe, "she's in the grade below me. The grade that fifteen-year-olds are in. I didn't think she was a twenty-year-old who couldn't pass her exams."

I snicker. Gabe's so funny; he might even be funnier than Hannah. Oh, *Hannah*! I haven't had a second to email her again, something better than *Everything will be OK, here's a stuffed owl with its head on the wrong way*. I will do it when I get home, even if I'm dropping with tiredness and it's five a.m.

We reach the edge of the field and Pete leads us into a dark little wood. He marches through it and we all follow like obedient ducklings.

It comes out into what looks like an industrial estate, and Pete heads down an alleyway toward a big concealed doorway.

Pete fiddles with the lock and carefully pushes open a heavy metal door, and we follow him in. We're in pitch darkness, but the air feels warm and there's a weird smell. Also a humming noise. *Where* is this? I follow Pete closely. It's *so* dark in here. I reach out and pinch his sweater gently. I expect him to tell me to get off, but he doesn't, and Gabe hangs on to me in the same way.

There's carpet underfoot that's so rough my sneakers are catching on it and making me trip. We take a few steps forward, then Pete suddenly turns right, and I stumble over the back of his foot. I fall forward, putting my hands out to catch myself, but there's nothing there and I'm falling and falling into darkness and I don't land on the floor—I land on a sloping pane of thick glass. My hands slap down on it first, smooth and cold, followed by my head. Hard.

As my forehead smacks against the glass, the most nightmarish thing I've ever seen looms at me: cold, pale skin, stone eyes, and rows and rows of teeth.

A shark.

It emerges silently out of the darkness and I think I'm going to die. I scream and scream and my head is throbbing. There's whooshing in my ears, and I slide down the glass until I'm crouching, wrapping my arms around my head to save myself from those teeth and then . . .

. . . nothing.

chapter 25

I open my eyes. I'm lying on the floor. The carpet is so rough it's like lying on Velcro. It's snagging my pants, and I notice in a dreamy way that it's giving me a wedgie.

My back is aching and I feel sick to my stomach, but there's something soft under my head, and cool hands are cupping my face.

"Lou? Lou?" I feel breath on my cheek; it's Gabe's voice. He turns to the others and says in a harder tone, "Call an ambulance."

"We can't!" That's Pete, sounding panicked.

"His dad will lose his job!" Roman is somewhere far above me.

"I don't care! Call an ambulance!" I've never heard Gabriel sound so angry.

"I'm here. I'm . . ." I'm *trying* to say, "I'm not dead and *please why shark?*"

"Oh god, Lou!" breathes Gabe, sounding like his old self again. I feel a weight on my shoulder: his head. I put my hand on his hair. I feel like I should be comforting *him*, not the other way around.

"Are you in pain?" he asks.

"No," I lie. To be honest, between the garbage can, the upturned bike, and now this, I am 87 percent pain, but whatever.

"The shark!" I pull myself into a sitting position. My stomach churns. "Was . . . did . . . ?"

"We're in the aquarium," explains Gabriel with a shaky laugh in his voice. The aquarium. Of course.

"You could've said!" I say in the general direction of Pete's voice.

"I wanted it to be a surprise," he defends himself, sounding uncharacteristically nervous.

I say heavily from the floor, "I was surprised."

I hear Roman give a tiny laugh, and I get to my feet slowly with Gabe's help.

"So now what?" I ask a little throatily. Standing up makes me feel like sick times sick, so I lean against a wall.

"Now," says Pete, his voice disappearing into the darkness, "this!" He turns on the lights in the fish tanks, and the water glows with a bluish light. Small schools of shining fish drift past the glass. It's the most beautiful thing I have ever seen.

We stand in silence and I find myself reaching for Gabriel's hand. To my surprise, Roman reaches for mine. It feels nice, like a family. I wonder if Roman and Pete are holding hands too? Best not to ask. We stare in silence until Pete breaks the moment.

"Now, what would you like to swim with?" he says, peering in to read the labels. "Koi carp, tuna fish, or—"

"Swim *with* the fish?" interrupts Roman. "I thought you said there was an empty tank!"

"Yeah, there was, but now there isn't." Pete brushes it off as if it's not important.

"Sorry, Peter, hate to be dull," chips in Gabe, "but could we have a few more details on this?"

Pete sighs as if Gabriel is being ridiculously fussy.

"There was an empty tank, but it is EMP. TY. No water in it. So just for tonight we've got to swim with a few fish. It's fine, they're totally harmless. Shall we try tuna? I had a tuna sandwich for lunch; I feel like it's one-nil to me already."

Well, someone's in a good mood, I think groggily. That may be the first joke I've ever heard him make. But . . . hang on.

"Pete," I say, "tuna fish are huge and bitey."

"No they're not," he corrects me. We turn toward the tank, and about twenty tuna fish slide past. They're the most thuggish-looking fish I've ever seen in my life.

"Yeah. They are," say Roman and Gabe in unison.

"Oh, for f—" Pete sighs and runs lightly up a flight of stairs I hadn't seen in the gloom.

There's some activity above us, and the top of the tank slides to one side. We watch as one pale foot and leg appear in the water, then another. There's a moment of calm, then suddenly *all* the fish race toward them. It's so quick I yelp with shock.

In a flash, Pete yanks his legs out of the water, but those fish moved so fast, I can't tell if he got bitten. They look furious, thrashing around at the surface of the water. I can't be sure, but I *think* one of them is chewing.

"Pete, man?" Gabe calls quietly upstairs. "You all right?"

No answer.

"You probably ate a close friend for lunch, Pete. They wanted revenge," I call up.

We wait a moment, sniggering quietly.

"OK, fine." Pete appears again at the top of the stairs, acting as if that never happened. He bounds downstairs. "Let's try another tank."

"After you, man," Roman says, smirking.

Several nibbles and a couple of harrowing near misses later (seriously, if you've got an octopus in a tank, *label it*; there's no point being modest), we finally find a tank near the back full of tiny brightly colored fish that seem more scared of us than we are of them. We agree that we can only practice the underwater stuff, none of the lifts above water, but these things all need work, and the boys sink to the bottom of the tank and begin.

It is arresting to watch, and that's not just my concussion talking. The boys float in perfect unison in the glowing blue water with fish drifting past them in bright flashes of color. It's the most calm and eerie thing I've ever seen and I feel a bit in love with all of them at that moment. Yes, even Pete.

I film their whole routine on my phone, and I get the perfect take. At one point an eel swims in front of them! Thankfully, the boys are too absorbed in their swimming to spot it or they would've freaked out. I watch the video as they're getting changed upstairs, and I'm completely absorbed.

I notice I have Wi-Fi, so I upload the video to YouTube and, after a moment's thought, I send Hannah the link. Maybe it'll be good for her to see that there's life outside camp, that there are cool things happening elsewhere. I don't tag the boys or add any hashtags; let's keep it secret 'til tryouts. Nothing but bad has come of Debs discovering our secret. I don't want any more obstacles.

I notice a new email from Han. I can only see the preview, which says, I can't do this anymore.

Hmm, is that in a dramatic "I'm running away" way, or more of a "time for a new attitude, I must stop being so hard on myself"?

I keep refreshing my email to try to make it open. I'm a little bit anxious; if Hannah's email is serious, I want to call Mom and ask for advice.

I'm engrossed in my phone and oblivious to everything around me when suddenly Roman grabs me by the arm and shoves me and we're running, stumbling on the carpet and feeling our way along all the cold glass tanks. I'm stubbing my toes and fingers, banging my head, and I don't know what's going on except I know I'm scared.

"Police!" Roman hisses at me, and I feel cold with fear. *I'm running away from the police?* What has happened to my life?

The boys are running faster than I can keep up, even Gabe. I'm still woozy from banging my head, and I fall a couple of times and scrape my legs, but Roman won't let me go. He drags me up each time and keeps pulling me. I'm glad, because my head is thumping again and I feel so dizzy—there's no way I could do this by myself.

Now I hear what we're running from: heavy footsteps and dogs behind us. Pete suddenly darts left. There's the sound of a door opening, and he lunges back and grabs my other arm, pulling me, Roman, and Gabriel in behind him. It's a storeroom, I think. It smells like bleach and I see mops, buckets, and a Henry vacuum just before Pete shuts us in and we lose the faint aquarium light.

We are crammed tightly together. The boys are pressed against me on all sides, and I can smell aftershave, sugary hair product, and a slight smell of sweat. We're shaking with the effort of trying to breathe quietly. My head is against Roman's chest, and I can hear his heartbeat. This is the closest I have ever been to a boy.

It's gone quiet outside and I hold my breath (as if that will help at all). I close my eyes, but this makes me dizzy, and I take a small half step back. I lose my balance, Ro grips my shoulder, and I'm grabbing at Gabe and Pete so as not to fall in a loud clatter of mops and buckets.

All four of us are sliding downward, slowly and gently. It would be funny if we weren't so scared.

We can't get caught. We'll be in so much trouble. I'll be grounded, no more training, no more friends. Pete's dad could lose his job. . . . Please, whoever you are, keep walking.

I can't hear anything. Just the sound of us breathing. I feel really sick, and the room is starting to spin.

Suddenly there's a bang as the door is flung open and we all recoil from a blinding flashlight. The pressure in my head gets worse; I can feel my pulse thumping in my neck, and I'm sliding farther, 'til I'm practically on the floor. Roman, Pete, and Gabe all look oddly far away, Pete's lips move, but I can't hear what he's saying. There's a rushing noise in my ears, and blackness creeps in at the edges of my vision to meet in the middle.

chapter 26

I wake up suddenly with a strange pressure on my chest. I can't move my arms. There's a rustling noise when I try. I realize it's because I've been the victim of a brutally hard tucking-in.

Why am I in the hospital?

I turn my head and see Mom. She's rummaging through her bag and looks like she's been crying. Lav is standing behind her, unrecognizably serious with faint mascara streaks down her cheeks. She catches my eye, and her eyes widen with surprise. What is going on?

Mom's head jerks up and she gasps at the sight of me.

"Oh, Lou!" She bends down to the bed and hugs me tightly. "What were you doing?" she breathes into my hair. She's gripping me hard, angry with relief. I haven't seen her like this since I was seven and decided to snooze in the garage for a few hours without telling anyone.

Mom doesn't let go and I'm breathing in her shampoo smell. I'm remembering the aquarium bit by bit.

"Where's my phone?" I ask stupidly.

"You're not getting that back in a hurry," comes a grim voice from the other side of the room. I've never heard Dad sound so strict. When I turn my head to look at him, my neck feels stiff and tender.

"I'm sorry I sneaked out." I can't keep turning my head to talk to Mom *and* Dad, so I address Dad and squeeze Mom's hand. "It wasn't Laverne's fault. I just needed to help the boys with their swim training."

"Was that it?" Mom asks.

"Yes, of course!"

"Of course nothing!" Mom's temper flares up. "You were found in a broom closet with two older boys and a man who left school last year. You were unconscious and covered in bruises! We had no idea what had happened!"

I touch my face. It feels puffy and hard, and even lifting my hand sends shooting pains down my side.

"Do you want a mirror?" Lav asks.

Dad clears his throat. Lav and Mom look over at him. He obviously doesn't think this is a good idea.

Lav makes the decision and hands me a little compact mirror from her handbag. I put it up to my face and then angle it down to see my neck and shoulders. The cuts and bruising don't stop. My face is black and blue. I have a cut lip and strange marks all over me. It looks like I've been fighting wild animals.

Shark! That makes me remember the shark, and I shiver.

"Are you OK?" Mom is watching me warily.

"Mom, this is all my fault."

"None of this is your—"

"No, I mean it *really* is—I snuck out, I fell off the garbage can," I say, pointing at my shoulder. "Then I tripped over a bike in the back yard, then at the aquarium I fell over and head-butted one of the tanks. I know I look like a horror film, but no one *hurt* me. This is all incredible clumsiness."

Lav is watching me, her mouth twitching as she fights a grin.

Mom still looks grim.

"Blame an upside-down bike if you want to blame someone."

Mom shoots a look at Dad, who protests. "How did this become *my* fault?"

"Are the boys in trouble?" I ask.

"Yes," the three of them reply in unison.

"Can I have my phone?"

"No."

"But . . ."

"NO."

"I need to speak to Roman, Gabe, and Pete! I'm coaching them for *Britain's Hidden Talent*, and the tryouts are days away. . . ." I trail off because Dad is shaking his head, eyes closed.

"No, Lou, there'll be no *Britain's Hidden . . . Thing*. The boys will be lucky if they're not expelled, or worse."

Cold and hot runs through me. I feel weak, like the last bit of hope just leaked away. This isn't going to be all right, is it? Everything's ruined.

chapter 27

Lou, hon, are you OK? We heard you got ARRESTED with Ro
Garwood and Pete Denners, that can't be true, is it?!! Want to
meet up after swimming training this week? All the girls were
saying that we should because we haven't seen you in
AAAGES!

Nic xx

Hi Lou, I just wanted to get in touch to see if you're OK. Call
me if you'd like to talk, I can't imagine how you're feeling but I
can listen.

Cammie says hi.
Melia x

Girls, this is Lou's mom. I have her phone until further notice.

the hospital discharges me first thing next morning, and a young
policewoman comes to our house later to drink coffee and point

a skeptical face at me. Annoying. Mom gets out the china we only use at Christmas. It's strange to see it on duty in October.

No one will listen to me and I'm starting to get really scared on the boys' behalf. I show the policewoman the garbage can and the upturned bike, like the crappiest guided tour ever.

I'm still not allowed to have my phone back. I totally forget about Hannah's unread email because I have so many different problems—worrying if the boys got expelled or, worse, if the police are involved. Anytime I try to Google the local news on our home computer, Mom is on me like a tuna fish on Pete's leg. Plus I have these big painkillers to help me sleep and they leave me groggy until the afternoon, so my days drift by in a frustrating blur.

I have to stay home from school for a couple of weeks to get over the concussion and "let things blow over," as Mom says. Saturday is the last public tryout. The day passes and despite my begging, there's no way I'm allowed to go.

Mom and Dad won't even let me leave the house. They only manage to stop me by telling me if I go and see the boys, they'll be in *even* more trouble, and then that really will be my fault. So I go back to bed and I cry until I fall asleep and I wake up with a face like a blister.

I wonder if the boys go to the tryouts without me. I bet they do. I have the most unreasonable parents in the world. Laverne reports back that:

a) People are shamelessly nosy and she's told them all to eff off, especially Cammie, who says she's "distrawn" (not even a word).

b) Roman is back in school, but she hasn't seen Gabe.

c) She's getting used to Amelia Bond's lack of a hairy face mole, but it'll be a long road.

I suppose I'd rather Roman, Gabe, and Pete went to the tryouts without me than miss out. But when I think about them reaching the final while I'm stuck at home, I feel left behind. I have serious FOMO.

I wonder how Gabe could've done this for a year. I start going nuts after three days. Mom eventually lets me out for a drive with Dad after I start chalking up my days of incarceration on the bedroom wall with Lav's eyeliner.

Victory! Though I have to buy Lav a new eyeliner.

And, with perfect timing, my aching back and nausea turn out to be not aquarium-related but, in fact, my first period. Mom brings me a hot-water bottle.

"It's been a memorable week," I tell her.

"It's still not as traumatic as my first period."

"Pffft. How many police were involved in *your* first period?"

"None, but I was dancing in the school play. In white pants."

She tucks me in with that horrible thought. I don't dare sleep in case I dream.

The next day I'm catching up on some homework that Mr. Peters dropped off. ("Lovely guy. Dark eyes," Mom said. "Bit skinny," Dad muttered.) With a stomach jolt, I remember Hannah's email. I cannot believe I haven't thought about her since the broom closet, but concussion is a funny thing, the doctor said. "Hilarious," I said, feeling my lumpy head.

I beg Mom for my phone. She's about to say no, but I tell her about Hannah's latest messages, about her getting more and more stressed and her parents putting loads of pressure on her. Dad comes downstairs and loiters behind me, making a sandwich and eavesdropping.

"I am going to look through your phone," Mom says, in a voice that expects me to argue.

"'Kay."

"Laverne would go nuts if you tried that," Dad mutters, head in the fridge.

I roll my eyes. "That's because she has boys begging her to go out with them, and all *I* have is an argumentative synchronized swimming team."

Mom leans against the counter and scrolls through my phone. I look at her face for reactions.

"Anything?"

"Your friends from the swim team want to know if you're OK, *babes*," she says wryly. "You've got two new emails from Hannah."

"Can I read them?" I say, getting up to look.

"No. Not after the week you've had." She begins to read.

Dad stands behind Mom and looks over her shoulder. Their faces become grim.

"What?" I demand. "Come on, she's my best friend!"

They read on. At one point, without taking his eyes off the screen, Dad reaches out and holds my hand. I think he forgets to let go, and I inwardly roll my eyes. It goes on awhile as he and Mom are bent over my phone, heads touching as they scroll through all the older emails, and still we keep holding hands. Am I going to have to drag him off to college with me? *Hi, guys, this is my dad, could you get the door? No, it's cool, we go through sideways.*

Finally they finish and they look up at each other. Their noses are practically touching and for a crazy moment I think . . . are they're about to kiss? They're not a couple. They had better not kiss. Plus Dad's still holding my hand!

Thankfully they don't kiss *and* he lets go of my hand. Double win.

"What's a thigh gap?" Dad asks. I explain.

"Back fat?"

"Um . . ."

"Maybe fat that is on your back?" Mom says patiently.

"Right."

Mom catches my eye. I suppress a smile. She holds my hand and looks thoughtful. "So. It doesn't look like Hannah is coping very well with the pressure. Or that her parents are being very helpful." She pauses.

"What?"

They're clearly thinking something about me. I just can't tell what. Maybe the usual—"I hope she's not going to get any taller."

"OK," says Dad in his I Have a Plan voice. This is usually the voice with which he announces his intentions for experimental pudding recipes.

He hands me my phone.

"Lou, you email Hannah and ask her what she wants to do. Tell her we can call her parents . . ."

"No," I interrupt him, "she will *flip out*."

"Lou, she has already 'flipped out.' She thinks back fat is important. So just be honest with her. And then?"

"Yes?"

"You can give me your phone back."

chapter 28

Dear Hannah, I'm so so sorry, I didn't realize you were going mental.

Hmm. Delete.

Hannah, I'm really sorry. I've been making new friends and I hadn't noticed you were . . .

Even worse. Delete!

Hannah, I'm sorry, I didn't realize you were finding training camp so hard. It sounds like a really difficult place. Do you want me to tell your parents? Maybe you could talk to the coaches about slowing down your training? I'm sure if you told someone you weren't happy, they would help you. It's easy to feel like winning is the only thing that matters, but I don't think

it is. Take it from a loser! I'm sorry I've been so slow to get
back to you—I've had a crazy couple of weeks. I'll tell you
more later. Please let me know you're OK!

Lots of love,

Weez xxxxx

It took me ages to phrase this, sitting at the kitchen table with
tea cooling in front of me. But finally I think I've nailed it. I press
Send, then hand my phone to Dad, who carefully puts it in a box.
He locks the box with a little key, which he gives to Mom, who pockets it with a smug face. Dad stands on tiptoes and pushes the box
onto a high shelf in the kitchen cupboard that not even I can reach.

He turns back and stands shoulder to shoulder with Mom. They
fold their arms—no one can take on Team Parent.

Almost immediately my phone makes a pinging sound and vibrates inside the box. Their faces drop.

"That's probably Hannah replying," I tell them, unnecessarily.
Dad sighs and goes back to the cupboard and Mom digs in her pocket
for the key.

It is Hannah.

DON'T SAY A WORD TO MY PARENTS. Seriously! This means
the world to them. But you're not a loser, you know you're
not. That video from the aquarium was amazing, I've shown it
to tons of people here! I'm OK. I just feel low at night, things
always seem better in the morning. Gotta go . . . we're all off
to the movies. Only joking, trainintrainingtraining. FML.

Xxxxxxxxx

That wasn't the answer I was expecting. I don't like how vague it is. Mom takes the phone, and she and Dad read the message.

"OK," says Dad. "But I'd be much happier if we told her parents."

"She'd be so angry at me. I already feel bad showing this to *you*."

"Keep talking to her," says Mom, and hands me back my phone. "I'm trusting you," she adds, hanging on to it a second longer than she needs.

I head upstairs and spend the rest of the day Googling all the things I haven't known for a couple of weeks. It takes ages. By the time I finished checking *distrawn* (knew it wasn't a word), Lav is back from school and flopping wearily down on her bed, shaking her homework out of her bag.

"Good day at school?"

She sighs. "People are still bugging me about you."

"Can't they find out from Roman?"

"I heard this girl, Camo—"

"Cammie."

"—trying to flirt it out of him. He was pretty rude to her."

I really enjoy that news, for several reasons.

I sigh and catch sight of my stomach. I lift my top up and look at it. It's less muscle-y than it used to be. Cammie once said, "That would be so hot. On a guy." She's good at insulting me in a way that sounds like a compliment. So I have to say thank you or else *I'm* rude.

I suck my tummy in and push it out as far as I can. Then suck it in again. Skinny. Fat. Skinny. Fat. Hate Cammie.

"What are you doing?" comes a wary voice from the other bed. I look over and Lav is staring at me over the top of a textbook. I pull my T-shirt down primly. Honestly, no privacy in this room.

"I have you on eating disorder watch, just so you know," she informs me. "You've been on it since the time trials."

"That's sweet," I tell her. "I have you on pregnancy watch."

"Ha ha," she says good-humoredly. She puts down her textbook and rolls onto her stomach. Dammit, *everything* Lav does is elegant. Probably because she has much less body to control. I'm so lanky, when I move, it's like trying to lead a school trip around the zoo—barely controlled chaos.

"I know you look different now that you're not training, but it's OK, all right?"

"OK."

"Don't you dare get an eating disorder. If you go bulimic, you'll rot your teeth. If you go ano, you'll get a hairy face."

"I *won't!*" I say, horrified.

"Uh-huh," she says authoritatively, disappearing back behind her textbook. "Your body goes fluffy everywhere, like granny's chin *all over.*"

I think for a second, then hand over my phone with a thread of Hannah's last emails. "Does Hannah sound a bit weight-obsessed to you?"

She skim-reads it. "Yes. Are you going to tell her parents?"

"I told Mom and Dad, but if we tell Barbra and Damian, what if they pull her out of the Training Camp? Then she won't get to be a swimmer and all her dreams will be ruined and it'll be all my fault because I *told*—"

"Lou, breathe."

"Sorry. It's very stressful to think about it. It must be worse to live it."

"Stop picking your lips, you'll make them bleed. Look, you made them bleed. Hannah sounds pretty messed up."

"Yeah, but I bet everyone there is messed up!"

She chucks me a tissue.

"Thanks," I say, dabbing my split lip.

"Well." Lav shrugs. "I would tell them."

"I think Dad wants to. Mom and I say no."

We both lie back on our beds.

"So it's a tie," says Lav.

"Hannah makes it three to two we don't tell."

"Hmmm."

I tap out a quick good night message to Hannah. It's so good to have my phone back.

I watch it send and I see she's read it immediately. Some dots appear—she's writing. They go, she's stopped. They pop up again, she's having another go. I watch the dots.

"Don't watch the dots." Lav says wisely. "It's a rule of dating."

I put my phone down. She'll reply tomorrow.

chapter 29

Drafts Folder

Hi Gabe, are you OK? I'm OK, I'm sorry, I don't know what happened.

Gabe, can we talk?

Hi Gabriel, what's going on? Everything is so weird here.

Hi Roman, I don't know if you want to talk to me but

Hey Pete

i haven't broken my word to Mom, I haven't *sent* any messages to the boys. I would, if only I could think of the right thing to say. Anyway, I'll be seeing them soon.

Yesterday, Mom and Dad said I can go back to school if I think it'll be OK. No, Mother, Father, bless your optimism, it will be *far* from OK. Lav says all anyone knows is that the three boys got arrested and I was there, and that could mean *anything*, right?

Bottom line: Loner Loser Lou Brown got three popular boys arrested. I can't see this raising my social standing much higher, but how much lower can it possibly go? I bet people will want gossip for a few days, then they'll forget about it, so I'll just keep my head down. Funny after I've spent half a semester desperate for anyone to talk to me.

I pack my backpack the night before, and I feel something bulky at the bottom. It's *Swimming for Women and the Infirm*. The spine is flaking away, it's sat forgotten at the bottom of my bag since our last training session. The musty old smell of it reminds me of late nights in the swimming pool, and I feel sad that all that is over. Even my shoe box full of twenty-pound notes makes me feel nostalgic; I'm not sure I'll ever have the heart to spend the money. Lav offers to take it off my hands if it's too emotional. So kind, I tell her. But no.

I wake up early the next morning and I'm eating cereal as Mom and Lav come downstairs. They give me supportive looks, but I just stare into my bowl—I'm not in a good mood. I sneak out *once* in fifteen boring nerdy years and all hell breaks loose. Because when I rebel, I really go in with both feet.

Dad gives us a lift. He pulls up in the school parking lot and Lav turns back from the front seat.

"Want to walk in together?"

"If that's OK."

"Of course."

She waits for me as I disentangle myself from the car and my backpack. I'm nervous and clumsy and I can feel people's eyes on me. Looking, not actual eyeballs. Gross.

When I finally step out of the car, my legs feel a little rubbery as Laverne and I walk toward the front doors. People are definitely staring, and I'm blushing already. But Lav doesn't peel away from me to join her friends. She walks me right to my homeroom, and luckily we bump into Mr. Peters in the doorway.

I feel like Lav hands me over to him like a package, but it's probably for the best. As I enter the homeroom, some people stop talking and stare at me, while others talk more urgently, possibly about me. I don't look good. My face is still a mess of bruises, and I have carpet burns on my hands and a nasty scab on my lip. I sit at an empty desk at the front rather than risk walking all the way to the back. I'm next to Mr. Peters, so no one dares to approach me.

The people at this school are the worst. It's either ignore you or stare at you. Find a middle ground, weirdos!

The bell goes off for the first class.

"Hey, is that a *bruise?*" some guy yells at my back as I race out of the homeroom, and I can hear a couple of girls gasp, scandalized but amused.

Three more years, Lou, I tell myself, hitching up my backpack and walking head down toward my history class. Three more years, take your exams, change your name to Trixie McCool, go to college, and deny Louise Brown ever existed, let alone went to an aquarium after hours.

I'm exhausted already. A week and a half in bed and I feel weak as a kitten. I snooze gently at the front of history with my Interested Face on. The teacher isn't convinced, but she leaves me alone today.

At my size, I'm not one of life's natural sneakers, but today I do my best. I skulk in the bathroom in the first break, then sit at the front for my next two classes.

At lunch I'm heading to the cafeteria, looking around for Roman and Gabe, but I don't see them anywhere. Instead I bump into Melia. She smiles, looks genuinely pleased to see me.

"Hey, you OK?" she asks, jumping straight in without any chit-chat. Seems odd, but then Cammie and the rest of them appear behind her, putting an end to any conversation.

"Oh my god, look at *you*!" drawls Cammie. "Who did that? Not Roman? Did he *hit* you? Were you in an accident?"

People are turning to look, exactly as she intended. Melia looks mortified.

"Cammie," she murmurs.

"What?"

"Just . . . forget it."

Well done, Melia, way to assert yourself. I take advantage of Cammie's being distracted to sneak past them and do the unthinkable.

I quickly buy a sandwich at the cafeteria and head to my old refuge, the library. I'm going to find the biggest book I can and hide behind it. If it's big enough, I'll build a fort and refuse to come out until it's time to go home. Immature, but that's my plan.

I turn into an emptier hall and I feel myself calming a little. Honestly, all this drama! The worst thing I did was lie to my parents and maybe scare a few fish. There wasn't half this much fuss when Lav snuck out to a party, trod on a nail, and ended up in the hospital, in sequined booty shorts, getting a tetanus shot. The injustice rankles.

Head down, I'm marching quickly down the hall. I turn a corner and I walk straight into Roman—I actually bang my face on him.

"Owb!" I say pitifully, pinching my nose. It tastes metallic, as if I might get a nosebleed.

"Sor . . ." Roman begins but falls silent when he sees it's me.

A mean voice in my head wonders if he'll say hi. Bearing in mind he didn't talk to me at school *before* I got him arrested and nearly expelled. But a less bratty voice reminds me how he held on to me when we were running through the aquarium and he didn't let go even when I was slowing him down.

"You look awful," he says, shocked.

A couple of boys from my grade turn into the hall, see us, and openly stop and stare.

Roman glares at them and they remember they were on their way to something very important, actually, and bustle past.

"I know I do. It's this new shampoo," I tell him.

Roman laughs. He never laughs at my jokes. Perhaps it's a pity laugh, but I'll take it. I feel sorry for myself. Every time I speak, my lips tug at the scab on my mouth. *Bleurgh.*

"How are you?" I venture.

"I've . . . been better," says Roman carefully. I feel like he's hiding something from me, and also . . . "Stop talking to my scab, please," I tell him.

"God, sorry." He smiles. He's so handsome when he smiles, but I'm not thinking about that right now. I'm preoccupied with something else.

"Where's Gabe?" I ask.

"Ill," Roman says, his friendliness cooling. "With the stress, he's ill again."

I feel like I've been kicked in the stomach.

"I . . . I'm so sorry."

"It's not *your* fault!" He seems almost angry at the thought.

"I know it's not my fault!" I retort. "I'm sorry for *him*, I mean. I like him, he's my friend. I don't want him to feel like he's got flu all the time and he's tired and his limbs ache and stuff."

"Did he tell you that?"

"Yes. Now, where do you live?" I ask, getting out my phone so I can type in the address. I'm going to go see him, I decide. Right now. Roman watches me.

"You want to see him?"

"Of course!" I say. "If that's OK?"

"I was just about to get a lift from Pete, if you . . . ?"

"Will Pete want to see me?"

"Oh, shut up," he says, grabbing me by the backpack and giving me a little shove. "We'll drop you back by the end of lunch."

Our strides match as we walk out to the parking lot together; I'm nearly as tall as him. I can see people watching us and I begin to feel pretty nervous.

This is one of the stupidest things I've ever done, and I've been really adding to that list this past couple of weeks. I'm cutting school with two boys who were recently accused of beating me up. In a closet. In an aquarium.

Pete is waiting in the parking lot in his Mini, having a cigarette. I guess we aren't training anymore, but I still feel a prickle of motherly irritation at him. He stares when he sees me, flicks it out the window, and gets out to say hi. I give him an awkward wave, and I'm shocked when he comes over and gives me a hug.

He squeezes pretty much every bruise I've got, but that's OK.

Roman opens the passenger door, flipping the seat forward for me.

(This is so cool! Or it would be if it weren't an emergency dash to the sickbed of someone I really care about.)

"Actually, do you want front or back, Lou?"

(And if it weren't physically impossible to get three lanky teenagers in a Mini.)

"Um."

I feel like the only way we'd all fit in is if we liquidized ourselves and someone poured us through the sunroof. So I take the backseat and we play a slow, careful game of Twister as eighteen feet of human being is folded up inside the car.

We get the giggles halfway through, and this helps nothing except it makes me feel a lot better. I don't remember the last time I laughed. I think it was pre-shark.

chapter 30

Lav
Are you OK? Millie says you cut school
with Roman and Pete? You are aware this
is the Worst Idea Ever?

Lou
Gabe's ill, I went to see him.
I'll be back by the end of lunch!

Lav
OK. Stay away from fish.

We get to Roman and Gabe's house—Ro lets himself in, Pete follows behind, clearly at home here, and I suddenly feel a bit shy.

It's bigger than our house, I notice as I walk in, but not as swanky as Hannah's.

"Gabe! Lou's here, are you decent?"

"Lou? Really?"

"Yes! Get dressed!" I call up the stairs. I hope his mom isn't in; that was dangerously close to flirty.

Gabe is dressed but sitting on his bed surrounded by stacks of books and a laptop. I don't hug him, because it feels weird—he's in bed. Instead, I sit on the end of the bed and squeeze his leg.

"How are you?" we ask at the same time, and laugh.

"Better."

"Better." (Golden rule: never too many words with boys, even really nice ones.)

The four of us sit and talk for a little. I have to ask them: "Did you go to the tryout? I mean it's cool if you had to go without me. Fine. Really."

They all look awkward. Roman speaks first.

"Me and Gabe were suspended. I thought we'd be expelled; the three us were nearly charged with assault. And then Gabe got ill and we barely noticed the day of the tryouts."

"I told my parents!" I protest, shocked. "I said the bruises were me being clumsy when I sneaked out and that I fainted because I was . . . coming down with something."

"What were you coming down with?" Gabe asks, and Roman and Pete look at me.

Of course, *now* I have their full attention. When I'm trying to teach them how to dive neatly, no one listens, but for this they're all ears.

"Girl," I tell Gabe. "I was coming down with a case of Girl Things."

"Are you going to get better?"

"No. It's terminal Girl. I may have to buy a dress."

"Anyway!" Pete interrupts. Clearly, he'd rather talk about getting arrested than my fascinating biology. Fair enough. "You were unconscious for hours."

"We were really worried," Ro says sweetly.

"Yeah, for us *and* you," Pete scoffs. "It looked like we'd abducted you and beaten you up. In an aquarium. Like weird, violent thugs."

"Did you not tell them the truth?" I ask.

They look at me.

"Hey, Officer," Ro begins. "We were practicing underwater synchronized swimming. . . . No, it's not technically a Thing. We made it up."

"And we broke into an aquarium . . ." Gabe adds.

"With a girl I only just discovered was a bizarrely tall *child* . . ." Pete splutters.

"Hey!" I protest.

". . . to fool around in a fish tank with some eels," Roman concludes.

"The police didn't believe you, then," I guess.

"It sounded so crazy, they drug-tested us!" Gabe says indignantly.

I can't help laughing. It does sound like a surreal excuse for breaking into an aquarium. Then I remember something that hasn't crossed my mind since the hospital.

"Hey! Want to see you guys swimming in the tank?" I ask. "I filmed it."

"No way!" Excited, they crowd around my phone, but it's being stupid and slow. The video is taking up too much memory.

"Hang on, I'll delete it."

"I want to *see* it!" Pete whines.

"No, it's cool, I uploaded it to YouTube. I didn't tag any of us in it," I add, seeing the looks on their faces. "No one from school will find it. You're still cool, guys, don't worry."

I find the URL in my history, click it, and leave it loading slowly, propped up against the window, and promise them they can watch it soon.

"You need an iPhone," Pete tuts.

"Not now I've lost my job," I tell him.

I catch sight of the time and realize I'm already running late for my afternoon classes. I have to get back! Just as I'm grabbing my backpack and Pete is getting his keys, there's a bang of the front door. Roman and Gabe look at each other and I can tell it's a parent.

I hold on to my backpack straps and feel nervous.

Light footsteps run up the stairs, and a small, elegant woman pops her head around the door. Her eyes go straight to me.

"Um, hello, I'm Louise, hi!" I blurt.

I feel so awkward—I wonder if she thinks of me as the person who got both her sons locked in a police cell. It was a bad night for me, but I bet it wasn't one for her family album either.

But as soon as Gabe and Ro's mom sees me, she steps across the room and hugs me gently. My bruises thank her for that.

"Are you OK?" she asks.

"I am, yes, thank you. I'm sorry everything . . ." I trail off, unsure how to finish that sentence.

"I'm sorry my boys were so irresponsible," she says. "I know they would never hurt you, *but* they were thoughtless and that caused you to get hurt."

Nicely put. I feel like she's untangled a knot in my head and I start feeling less guilty.

"I have to get back to school," I say. "I'm sorry!"

"Yes, of course." Pete holds up his car keys.

"Can I jump in and pick up some homework?" Gabe asks. "I really need to get out of the house."

"OK," says his mom, but she points a warning finger at Pete. "Drive. Carefully."

Gabe gets up stiffly and pulls a hoodie on. We all head downstairs, me first. I don't want him to feel shy about me seeing how weak he is. We head out to the car.

Gabe gets into the car first and I clamber into the backseat next to him, trying not to shove my butt in his face.

Roman looks at him anxiously. "Are you cold?"

"I'm fine," Gabe protests, but Roman chucks a blanket over his legs anyway. I tuck it in tightly so he can't move his legs, just to be annoying.

We're pulling out of the driveway (really slowly, in case Gabe and Roman's mom is watching) when she appears at the front door, waving my phone, which I left on the windowsill.

"Thank you!" I shout as she throws my phone through the window. "Nice to meet you!"

"I'll feed you next time!" she promises.

I grab my phone as it falls, and I see that the video has uploaded.

"Ah, look, here you are!" I say, and hand it forward. "This is you guys in the aquarium." Ro holds up the phone so that he and Pete can see it in the front and Gabe can see it in the back.

The video begins. And the boys in the front suddenly lean forward, blocking our view of the screen.

"Hey!" I protest.

"Down in front!" Gabe prods his brother in the back.

"Wait. But . . ." Pete looks at Roman, then at us. "We have over a million views."

We all bang heads as we lurch forward to see. . . . One million three hundred twenty-two thousand views.

"How . . . just *how*?" They all turn to me. It wasn't me—I have barely any social media. It must all be down to other people. I look on my phone. It was chosen as a Pick of the Week on a couple of websites, some people stumbled upon it and shared it, an actor tweeted about it, a DJ and a model liked it. . . . Basically, my little video traveled around the world, rubbing shoulders with the stars, while I was moping in bed with a hot-water bottle. Mental.

Roman starts whooping and banging his seat, the roof, Pete. . . . We all join in until Pete's poor little Mini is rocking and making noises of complaint.

I glance round to see if their mom has heard us. I want to tell Mom and Dad and Lav, but first I hug our fame to us—just for now it's our secret.

"Who cares about *BHT*, huh?" I say.

"Damn right," says Pete. "A million people have seen us already."

"Thanks to you, Lou," says Roman unexpectedly. "You're a genius. I don't know how you came up with those ideas. I'm sorry we never said it before."

"I had help. From you guys and . . ." Feeling mischievous, I pull *Swimming for Women and the Infirm* out of my backpack and flip it open. I can see from their faces that they recognize some of the moves.

"Never tell anyone about that," Roman says firmly, and Pete agrees.

"Deal," I say cockily. "If you pay my library fine. It's massive."

Gabe is still looking at my phone.

"Don't look at the comments!" I warn him.

"Why not?" Pete asks.

"Because Life Lessons 101, don't read what people say about you on the Internet?"

"Wimp," he scoffs, and scrolls down.

The comments are amazing. There are a couple of mean ones, and some people accuse us of fish abuse, but mainly they say Roman is gorgeous, Gabe's cute, and Pete's got massive feet. I'd never noticed that before, and I sneak a peek but he catches me looking.

"Size fifteen," he says a little huffily.

When we get tired of reading nice things about the boys and the routine (which takes a while), we all sit back in our seats and breathe a happy sigh. One. Million. Views.

"At least something good came out of the aquarium," I say.

"Worth getting arrested for," Pete agrees.

"And suspended," Roman joins in.

"Relapsing," Gabe adds.

"I'm still having nightmares about sharks," I lie. "So I win."

"School!" Gabe says, catching sight of the time, and Pete starts the car again and prepares to drive off. A second later he stops, frowning at his rearview mirror.

"Is your mom OK?" he asks. We all look behind us to see Roman and Gabe's mom chasing down the road after us. But this time she's waving the house phone.

"I don't know," says Roman, "hang on." He gets out of the car and jogs back to her. She gives him the phone and watches him take a call.

Pete goes to join them, leaving me and Gabriel sitting in the back of the car like a pair of muppets.

"The seat in front of me doesn't tip forward, but I think yours does," he says.

"That's all right," I yawn. I suddenly feel so tired. I guess it's been my first day out of bed in a week, and a lot has happened.

Gabriel rests his head on my shoulder and I rest my head on top of his. The silence goes on and on, but it doesn't get awkward. It's the most relaxed I've ever felt with a boy. I close my eyes. Even though I'm wondering what's happening outside, the heat of the car is making me drowsy.

Suddenly Pete and Roman are rocking the car, opening the front doors and shouting. It's the worst way I've ever been woken up, *including* the time Gran's cat puked on my forehead. Gabe and I both yelp and clutch each other. I let go of him very quickly as Pete and Roman smirk at us over the backs of the front seats.

"That was *Britain's Hidden Talent* on the phone. They saw our video, they love it, and they want us to come and try out! We have one more chance! I told them we have nothing to swim in," adds Roman before I can open my mouth, "and they say don't worry about it, they'll figure it."

I'm awake now, really awake, and I'm clutching Gabe's arm again.

"Wh-when?" I splutter.

"This weekend. We have four days."

I look across at Gabriel. He's smiling but already shaking his head.

"I won't be well enough," he says. My stomach sinks and I try not to show how disappointed I am. Just for one second it was like the last terrible week had never happened.

"Hey," I say weakly, "that's OK. It's just a dumb TV show for—"

"No." He interrupts me. "*You* swim for me. You have to, you know everything I do and you're a stronger swimmer anyway."

"But . . . but," I stammer.

"No buts. And you chose the Lycra, so it's your own fault you have to wear it."

I'm dry-mouthed with shock. But there's a familiar feeling in my stomach. A tangy, bubbly feeling. It's competitiveness. Hello, old friend.

The boys pile back in the car and we play drum and bass loudly, shouting along to it with happy whoops. There are no words to drum and bass; it's basically noise, so you just shout what feels right. It's a lot of fun. Especially when it starts raining hard and the thundering on the roof adds to the deranged feeling.

I breathe in deeply. This car smells of hair product and empty cheese curl bags. I reflect that I will never smell a cheese curl again without feeling nostalgic for this autumn with my friends.

And then I think that that was quite a weird thought and wonder how many brain cells you lose when you head-butt a shark tank.

chapter 31

Roman

Lou, I just realized you can't wear
Gabe's competition outfit, can you?

Lou

No, Ro, because I am a girl and . . .

Gabe

Awks.

Lou

That's cool. I have tons of bathing suits.
If you're sure you can't do it, Gabe?

Gabe

Sorry. You'll have to be the TV star.

Lou

I feel sick.

Pete

Think how we feel, we've got to lift you out of
the water now. You're like a Gabe and a half.

Roman

What a gent.

Lou

Swoon.

Gabe.

No. More. Fainting.

I get back to school half an hour late for my afternoon class, but it's English and I guess Mr. Peters assumes I was skulking in the library, trying to stay out of the way of gossip, because he taps his watch but doesn't mention it. Mom's right—he does have nice eyes, I think, grateful I'm not in any more trouble.

Teachers seem to be lenient on me all week, probably because my face still looks so battered. This is useful because I'm back to nodding off in classes, thanks to swim training every evening. Thankfully, we're managing to avoid Debs, as I'm sure she'd book the pool *every* evening if she knew we were still planning to compete.

Gabe persuades Pete to be a "honey trap," which I find very funny once I find out what it means. Basically, Pete has to do some tactical flirting with Cammie to find out what she and her team are up to. Practicing every evening in some swanky private members' pool that Nicole's dad owns. Whoop-de-doo for them. It leaves the public one free for us at least.

I hear from Gabe who hears from Ro that Pete might go on a date with Cammie. He thinks she's "really sweet." Ha. Sweet like a *snake*, I tell Gabe, and hope the message heads back the way it came.

I suggest we train first thing in the morning, too, but wow, if I thought Pete was a grumpy ass normally, that's nothing compared to how he is in the morning. We all agree to never do that again. As Gabe says, bundled up in sweaters and watching from the bench, the routine will look a little off if one of the swimmers has killed the other two.

Pete started driving me home from practice. Dad was skeptical at first, but Pete waits until I get to the front door and then waves before driving off. Dad seems to appreciate the etiquette.

We're just coming back from our last practice when my phone rings. It's Lav. She doesn't bother to say hi.

"Lou, have you heard from Hannah?"

"No," I say, and then think. "Actually, I haven't—since I asked if I should tell her parents." I start to feel hot with guilt. "It's just so much has happened—"

"Someone's called the house phone a couple of times but hung up when we answered. Have you got any missed calls from her?"

"No," I say. *Just* as my phone starts beeping with messages. I take it away from my ear to look. Six missed calls from Hannah. Argh. Great timing. We get no reception poolside. "Hold on, let me try her."

I hang up on Lav and call Hannah, but it goes straight to voice mail. I try a few more times, but either her phone is off or she's poolside too (highly likely). I glance up. We're at my house, and the boys are all looking at me. I briefly explain.

We pull into the driveway and I jump out. To my surprise, the boys follow.

"Can we do anything?" asks Roman, helping Gabe out of the car.

"I don't know," I say honestly. "I don't know what's going on." I'm fumbling for my keys. Mom's already opening the front door. "Mom!" I say. "This is Roman and Pete and Gabriel."

"We met," she says icily. "At the police station."

Well, *there's* an introduction. I look back at the boys. Pete and Roman smile like they've been sick in their mouths, but Gabe sways a little and puts his hand on the wall to steady himself. Mom steps forward.

"Come in," she says, and I think it's going to be all right.

Meanwhile, the Hannah situation is so far from all right that *all right* is just a tiny dot on the horizon. Apparently, she finally spoke when she last called the house phone—she told Mom that she just wants to leave the training camp but doesn't want her parents to know.

"So she's going to run away?" I ask, baffled. "But surely the camp would call her parents as soon as they realized she was gone. And where would she go if she didn't go home?"

"She's not herself," Mom says. "She sounds completely overwhelmed and panicked. I'm worried she might do something stupid. I'm sorry, Lou, but we need to tell her parents. Your dad's on the phone with them now."

Poor Han. As soon as my life improves, hers goes to hell, and I'm having too much fun to notice. Bad friend.

Mom makes everyone a cup of tea and forces Gabriel into a couple of sweaters.

We're all squeezed into the tiny kitchen. I'm sitting on the countertop with Lav perched on the fridge while the boys loiter in whatever space they can find. Dad is on the phone, pacing around the living room. I feel reassured with him in control; he's always been good with Hannah's mom. He said his tactic has always been to show no fear and try not to blink.

Mom picks her way through boy limbs to stand next to me. I rest my chin on her head and hug her. She feels small like this, but she still smells of Mom—moisturizer, dry shampoo, and fabric softener.

"I'm glad you're not at the camp!" she says. I give a little shaky laugh. I feel the same.

"Glad I have slow arms?" Debs would have a fit if she could hear us.

"Yes, Goldfish," Mom says into my hair.

We break apart. Gabe pretends to get sick into his sweater.

Dad has now paced out into the yard. He looks annoyed and is gesturing forcefully. He accidentally deadheads a few roses.

"I wonder if they're angry at us for not telling them sooner?" Mom wonders. "He'd better not punch my geraniums."

She remembers the boys suddenly.

"You know what you need?"

"I'm OK on sweaters, thank you," says Gabriel, a little muffled.

"Soup!" she declares, and heads for the cupboard. "Now, if I mix tomato and vegetable, will it be nice?" she muses.

"No," everyone answers.

Only Mom could ruin canned soup, this is why Dad does all the cooking.

A few minutes later we're all drinking soup out of mugs because there are too many people in here to open the cutlery drawer. When I finish taking another slow sip, I can see Dad hanging up and stomping across the lawn toward us.

"Uh-oh," I say.

Dad comes through the doorway with a halo of cold air and the smell of grass clinging to him. He takes a deep breath and looks at the phone.

"Hannah's parents think she's being 'melodramatic,'" he tells us. We all do Big Eyes of surprise at him and then each other.

"What? Did you tell them about the emails?" I demand.

"We sent them over," Dad says. "They read them while I was on the phone, but they chalked it up to teenage angst and a bit of jealousy on *your* part. Apparently, this is Hannah's chance of a lifetime, and she has to stay there and tough it out. I said I think she's actually quite ill, and if not she will be soon, but they're not listening."

I thought Hannah's mom and dad would flip out and that I'd be in trouble for not telling them earlier. I should have remembered they're weirdos.

"Then *we* have to go and get her," I say. It's a crazy plan, but it's the month for that, and of course we have to—we're the only people who will know her mom and dad are officially Awful. "Essex to Dorset isn't *that* far, surely?"

Everyone looks at me.

"Not that far," I persevere. "I mean, I'm not planning to walk it. I'll need a lift, but . . ."

Mom runs a finger over her eye. "I don't know what to do that'd be best," she says, sounding uncertain. Very unlike her.

"I'll drive to Dorset," Dad declares, "if Hannah's dad won't." This is very unlike him. Bold, bossy, and a bit competitive. Mom looks gratefully at him. Everyone's gone crazy this evening.

"We'll come," says Roman unexpectedly.

"Ah, now I don't think that's a good idea after your recent brush with the law, son," says Dad, not unkindly.

"What if you need some muscle?" says Pete, getting to his feet and looking suddenly very manly.

"That's why I'm taking Louise," says Dad.

Pete looks stubborn, "I don't want to be in the way, but I'd like to help. After the trouble we've already caused you."

Dad gives him a nod, and Mom says, "Not Gabe." Gabe doesn't object. He has dark circles under his eyes and is resting his chin on his hands. Mom will drive him home and explain to his parents where Roman went. She asks if she needs to call Pete's parents, but he laughs at the thought. I can't imagine Pete Senior is a stickler for bedtimes.

Roman, Pete, Dad, Lav, and I all pile into Dad's car and head off down the highway. My stomach is fizzing with excitement. I'm worried about Hannah, but I'm so glad we're finally actually dealing with it—and I can't wait to see my friend.

Plus it is *so cool* heading off on a rescue mission late at night! There's Dad and Pete in the front, with me, Lav, and Roman in the back. Lav's in the middle because she's the smallest. She's sharing a blanket with Roman; they make a really beautiful couple. I catch her eye in the rearview mirror and she gives me a prim face that makes me smile into my scarf.

Plus we're driving all the way to Dorset. It's like three hours there and three hours back! This is actual vacation driving, and it feels a little like a vacation—everyone's tired and eating sandwiches out of Saran Wrap.

I keep calling and calling Hannah, but her phone is still off. I remember her writing if it weren't for me and Candy Crush, she'd chuck her phone. I feel guilty. I haven't been in touch as much as I should lately. I text her.

Don't run, we are coming for you.

I realize too late that that sounds threatening.

PRISON BREEEAAAK!

After about an hour's driving, we stop at a gas station to grab fuel, chips, and cookies. Within a couple of minutes all the snacks are gone and we're picking the crumbs out of our hair and laps. Roman and Lav are being very helpful to each other with this, *so* predictable. Well, they'd better not come running to me if feelings get hurt.

"Um," says Pete.

"Yes?" says Dad.

"Is Hannah a . . . is she . . . what size is she?"

God, is *everyone* looking to get a date this evening?

"Lou, what would you say?" says Dad tactfully.

"She's like me. Maybe bigger," I tell Pete.

"Outstanding," he says. "Because there isn't a seat for her. We brought one too many people for a rescue attempt."

We all think about this.

"OK," Dad says finally. "If she's not nuts, we leave her there. And if she's really nuts, we strap her to the roof rack."

"Dad!" Lav slaps his little bald spot from behind.

"Hey!" he protests. "I'm a hero on a rescue mission. Show some respect and unwrap me a toffee."

chapter 32

We drive for a couple more hours, listening to a lot of songs that only Dad knows. There's a deep sigh of relief when we get near and he turns off the radio "to concentrate." Finally his GPS says we're there. It looks like a massive stately home. I had no idea the Training Camp was this plush; it looks like Hogwarts! A month ago this would've made me so jealous. I'm glad Hannah was too engrossed in her thigh gap to mention it.

The building is set back from the road, down a driveway with large iron entrance gates open in front of us. Dad hesitates, then turns slowly in. We look around for a security guard in a hut or a sign that says *Reception, Visitors This Way*, but there's nothing.

We crunch up the dark gravel driveway.

"I feel like we shouldn't be here," I whisper.

"Well, I'm not turning back now," says Dad.

"Should we turn the lights off in case we wake everyone?"

"Good idea," says Lav.

Dad turns his headlights off and we keep inching forward over the gravel.

"*Now* we look like burglars," Lav whispers in my ear. She has a good point. I hope the boys aren't about to be arrested for the second time in a month.

There's a sudden clunking noise and the car jolts to a halt. It's really spooky in the car with darkness all around.

Dad makes a puzzled sound and turns the lights back on. Everyone screams with fright at the woman standing in front of our car.

We bumped into a statue. It's a stern-looking woman holding a jug on her head. (No wonder she's moody. In my opinion, she's using all the wrong muscles. Must be agony.)

Dad reverses slowly . . . and she comes with us! Everyone makes a "Gah!" of shock. It looks like some piece of her is snagged on the front of the car. This rescue attempt is rapidly going wrong.

"Did anyone see that *Doctor Who* episode, 'Blink'?" Lav asks, and everyone says, "*Lav!*" crossly. Which I guess is a yes.

Pete tuts and gets out to deal with Moody McJug. She's pretty awkward to move, and he obviously doesn't want to break the arms or the jug, so we see him hesitate for a moment and then grab a boob with each hand.

There's a snort of laughter from the car. He gives us a look over her shoulder like, "Oh, grow up," but NO! Not gonna. Sorry.

Roman gets his phone out and leans forward to take photos. Pete unhooks her from the front of the car with a scraping noise that makes Dad wince. Pete gets back in the car, bringing a waft of cold air with him.

"Did you get her number?" I ask. He gives me a sniffy silence while everyone sniggers. We continue up the driveway. I try calling

Hannah again, suddenly realizing that this rescue mission is going to be extremely difficult if our damsel in distress has calmed down and gone to bed.

It rings! She picks up.

"Lou!" she whispers. She sounds like she's got a cold.

"I was so worried. Where were you?" I say. "Have you started running away or are you still there—I mean, *here*? Do you want to come home? You don't have to. We can turn around and go back, but . . ."

Lav is making "slow down" gestures. There's a silence from the other end of the phone.

"Are you here?" Hannah says as if she can't believe it.

"Yes!"

"With my mom and dad?" she asks, but thankfully she doesn't wait for an answer. "Yes! I want to come home."

"Can you see us on the driveway?" I'm whispering now too. I can hear her moving, pulling back a curtain.

"That's not my mom's car. Why did you come in a different car?"

Now is not the time to say, *Han. Bottom line, your mom and dad are awful. Sorry. Not all bad news, though, since mine are champions and we can share.*

"Um. It's my dad's. Tell you in a minute. Can you come out? Are you going to tell them you're leaving?" I say.

"I'll leave a note."

"It's not you, it's me?" I suggest, and she gives a little giggle.

Dad's mouthing something at me.

"Han, do you want Dad to come in and talk to your coach or something?"

"I can't face it. I will, but right now I just want to come home."

"OK. Meet you at the front door?" We hang up.

Lav and I get out of the car. Roman and Pete make to follow, but Lav stops them. "We'll go," she says. "She doesn't know you." The boys see the sense in that and sit back.

"Be quick, girls," hisses Dad. "This doesn't feel superlegal."

"It's OK, Dad," I tell him. "I watched a lot of TV crime shows."

We creep across the gravel, Lav holding me tight by my upper arm and guiding me toward the front door. I have terrible night vision, as a rainwater barrel and an upended bike can confirm. I still manage to trip over a couple of tiny statues.

"Stop that," Lav hisses in my ear. "Not again."

This tickles me, and we're both snickering quietly when the big wooden door creaks open and Hannah is standing there, silhouetted in the dim light from the hallway.

We stop laughing—she looks bad. This is coming from me, who's covered in scabs and bruises. She *still* looks worse. Thin and pale, with dark circles under her eyes to rival Gabe's. She's buckling under the weight of her bag.

I look to Laverne. I don't know what to say. I am fifteen. This is one of those times when I want to say, "Sorry, but I am a *child*, so I'm going to bed to watch *The Simpsons* and dip some cookies in milk. If I can just leave you guys to tidy up this rather adult mess? Bye."

Lav doesn't let me down. Her extra year of seniority steps up, and she reaches out a hand to Hannah.

"Han, this place looks lame. How about we go home?"

Han gives a small noise, half laugh, half sob. Laverne takes her bag and I put my arm around her and we all head back to the car. I can see the boys are pretending not to stare. I bet they thought this would be more action-adventure, less emoshe.

As we walk, I can feel how skinny Hannah has become. Dad flashes the car lights at us, and I wave back. He flashes again, more rapidly. Lav and I look at each other and wave at him again. Is he being cutesy? A time and a place, Dad?

He points behind us with big eyes. He's struggling to get his seat belt off. We look over our shoulders and squint to see, running silently over the grass, two *massive* guard dogs.

All three of us jump and scream uselessly, then start running toward the car, but we're running on gravel, which is slow. Lav is carrying a suitcase, and I'm basically carrying Han, who weighs less than the bag but is a more difficult shape, and there is *no way* we're going to make it.

My legs feel like water. Are guard dogs trained to kill? Bite, anyway, definitely, right? Dad's car is now tearing toward us, spewing up gravel as he makes a sharp turn and cuts between us and the dogs.

Roman grabs me by the arm in a familiar grip and bundles Hannah and me into the backseat while Pete shoves Lav in the front and dives in behind her.

Thump.

Thump.

We all wince as we realize that was dog versus car.

Dad pulls the car around in a wide sweep, and we race toward the gates. In the mirror we see the dogs giving chase again and two security guards bringing up the rear.

One of them takes something out of his back pocket and points it at the car. A red dot appears on the rear windshield.

"He's got a gun!" cries Lav, and everyone screams in terror and flattens across their seat. I feel Roman's protective arm over my neck, which is sweet but surprisingly painful as my knees dig into my eyeballs. When nothing happens, I sit up slightly, pushing his arm away.

"He does?" I ask. We all sit up, Dad keeping an eye on the gates but feeling around with one hand to check that everyone's all right.

"No!" says Han with a wobbly little laugh, and we all relax.

"No," says Pete, "it's a remote gate thing." We look at where he's pointing, and the massive iron gates, wide open a minute ago, are now closing.

"HANG ON!" yells Dad, flooring the accelerator. The wheels spin uselessly, flinging up gravel behind us, and I feel a moment's concern for the guard dogs, who are having a really bad day at work. Then we suddenly roar forward at a stately twenty miles per hour and burst through the gates, losing both door mirrors in the process.

"Sorry!" Dad yells out of the window as the rest of us cheer and whoop and bang on the roof.

"Can we go back for my mirrors?" Dad asks.

"No," I tell him, "that's the coolest getaway ever. Let's not ruin it by creeping back, like, 'Hi guys, did I leave my phone charger behind?'"

"Don't worry, Mr. Brown," Pete pipes up. "My uncle's a mechanic. He'll hook you up."

We drive back through the night, slowly because it's dark and rainy and Dad has to lean forward over the wheel to stare intently at the road.

"Hannah, this is Roman and Pete. They're the synchr—the swim team I mentioned." (I still can't quite call them a synchronized swimming team without imagining them in flowery rubber swimming hats. It would make this "prison break" seem so much less cool.)

Lav calls Mom, Roman and Pete call their moms, and I see

Hannah take out her phone and look at it thoughtfully. It has fourteen missed calls from me and *one* from "Home."

"So . . . my parents didn't believe you?"

Dad peers even harder at the road. Roman and Pete become very interested in the interior compartments of the car. Pete even opens the glove box with an engrossed air, like, "A box for gloves, eh? Well, this I must see. . . ."

"Well, they thought maybe it wasn't as bad as it seemed," I say diplomatically.

"They need their bloody heads knocked together," says Dad, less so. "Don't worry, Hannah," he adds, "you can call them in the morning and stay with us as long as you need to. My wife is very accommodating to waifs and strays. Me for one."

Lav reaches across Roman and pinches my leg.

"Wife," eh? In-ter-esting . . .

On the way home we swing into a twenty-four-hour drive-thru. I get a Big Meal and shake my fries into the side of my burger box, then put it over Hannah's lap and mine equally. She doesn't eat a lot, and she chews in a dry-mouthed way. That's OK, baby steps.

I want to talk to her about everything, but not in front of Roman and Pete. I turned up with cool new friends, and I don't want her to think I've told them all about her. She's still my best friend. I squeeze her hand.

I don't remember much more of that night; it's a blur of steamed-up windows, the rumble of tires, and the farty smell of old burger. I remember being helped out of the car and waking up just long enough to check that Hannah was all right. But my head was starting to throb and my aquarium bruises were aching. It was a relief to crawl into bed.

chapter 33

I wake up in a strange position on the edge of my bed. I can tell I haven't had enough sleep, and there's a dampness to the air that screams, IT'S TOO EARLY, GO BACK TO SLEEP!

I turn my head slowly and . . . ARGH! I'm nose-to-nose with Hannah, her eyes shining in the dim light. I laugh silently and she smiles.

"Sorry," she mouths.

I whisper slowly and carefully, "Are . . . you . . . less . . . crazy?"

That does make her laugh. She catches herself before she makes a noise. "I feel much less crazy," she says. "Those boys were cool."

"My boyfriend and my ex-boyfriend," I explain.

She grins.

"I am offended," I tell her, "that you didn't believe that for a *second*."

Lav croaks from the other side of the room, "If you don't shut up, I'm taking you both back to the nuthouse."

"Sorry, Lav."

"Sorry."

* * *

hours later, I wake up with a start. There's movement in the house. I can hear people talking in hushed voices and moving around in the kitchen.

"Want some breakfast?" I ask Hannah, and then wince. Bit tactless.

"OK" she agrees, "but aren't your tryouts today?"

Yes, they *are*. Oh, *that's* why we're up so early! In fact, are the boys still here? I race downstairs to see what's happening and bounce into the kitchen.

Pete and Roman are leaning against the sink, dressed in my father's clothes. It looks like they're heading to a My Dad–themed fancy dress party. Gabriel is sitting at the kitchen table, busy on his phone. He must've just come over. Mom is loading the dishwasher and Dad is loading up the car. How weird. I had a sleepover with Roman and Pete, apparently.

If you'd have told me last semester that this would be in my future, I would've given you a glass of water and made you lie down.

Pete catches sight of me and stares, his jaw dropping. Well, I coiff my big hair demurely, and they *are* nice pajamas. Thanks for noticing, Pete.

"Why are you not dressed and ready?!" he bellows at me.

"What sort of a coach *are* you?" Ro joins in.

"One who had four hours' sleep!" I yell back, but I'm already racing up the stairs.

I'm glad Mom and Dad saw that; after all their worrying about me hanging out with older boys, they can see I've just ended up with three bossy employers.

I jump in the shower and spot Lav's face wash. Maybe I'll make a bit of effort today; we might get on TV! There's a sudden banging on the door. I freeze, midlather.

"Are you using my face products?" comes Lav's voice from the hallway. It's eerie. How does she know? What a useless psychic ability.

"No-ooo," I lie.

She's not fooled. "Avoid your eyes and pay particular attention to your jawline. I've noticed that's where you get break-outs." Charming. But I do what she says with careful, unfamiliar gestures.

Showered, I sprint out of the bathroom and into my bedroom, yelling, "CLOSE YOUR EYES, CLOSE YOUR EYES!" as I whip off my towel, pull on my bathing suit, and go to grab some clothes from my drawer. But the drawer is empty.

If Mom has washed the few items of clothes I own *together*, then I'm in my newest nightmare and going to *BHT* with nothing on.

Hannah is lying in bed, watching me panic.

"All my stuff is dirty, but you're welcome to it." She points at her bag. Creased clothes are spilling out of it as if the bag's puking. That is my last resort.

I run my eyes all over our messy room, vainly trying to find something I own before I have to beg Lav for help. She has been very nice lately, but I doubt she'll lend me something to wear. The last time she did, everything got covered in blood and mud and was cut off me in the hospital.

"Come on, Lou!" shouts Dad from downstairs. Well someone's really getting into the spirit of things—only two weeks ago he was very lukewarm about my swim club.

"INNA MINUTE!" I yell.

"You're not as muscle-y as you used to be," Han says, watching me.

"Good thing, bad thing?" I ask, because if now is the time for a heart-to-heart about body image, we have to do it *fast*.

"Good thing," she says, sitting up and pinning back her hair. "You actually look like a gii-iirl." *Eurgh!* I make a joke-disgusted face and she makes it back. When we were in swim club, the worst thing to happen to a swimmer's times were boobs and hips.

Which reminds me.

"I got my period," I tell her.

"Oooh." She looks intrigued. "Was it . . . OK?"

I pause, thinking about the aquarium, the hospital, and the police. It's probably a story for another time. I'm sure most periods are less dramatic.

"Are you coming to *BHT*?" I ask. "We'll line up for about a hundred hours, so I can tell you then."

"My life." She rolls her eyes. "I get to choose between lining up in the rain talking about periods or seeing my parents."

"Good luck with your parents."

She makes a jokey grim face and tells me she'll come and meet us afterward. Then she grabs a towel, and heads for the bathroom, walking past Lav, who's standing in the doorway with a pile of clothes in her arms.

"OK," Lav begins, looking uncharacteristically nervous, "don't yell at me. I kept the receipts, but . . . I-took-your-money-out-of-your-shoe-box-and-bought-you-new-clothes. Are you angry?"

"No way, I *hate* shopping! Gimme!"

"How can anyone hate shopping?" Lav wonders, as if I'm a constant mystery to her.

I start searching through the clothes. "You haven't got me anything in pink or a *dress*?"

She's shaking her head scornfully. Sure, she's not an idiot.

I put on a pale green shirt; it's crisp and smells like a shop. Then I try to pull on some jeans. Oh, Lav. Skinny jeans?

"You have to lie down and pull yourself into them," she explains. I give her a hard look, lie down, and haul myself into the jeans. I bet there are bank vaults easier to get into.

"They'll look nice," she reassures me as I squirm on the floor. "You have a good body."

"You say that like I found it in a ditch," I grumble, but finally I'm in my denim prison and racing for the door when Lav slams it shut and positions herself in front of it.

"Two minutes," she commands, and I'm too surprised to argue. She comes at me with her hands up like a cartoon bear and runs that oil stuff through my hair again. Then she holds me hard by the chin, and a mascara wand is suddenly darting at my eyes.

"La-av," I whine, "I have to swim."

"It's waterproof," she sighs, and finally releases me to race down the stairs.

Mom, Dad, and the boys are waiting impatiently in the hallway.

"Pete's so jittery he's spilled two cups of tea," Dad says. "So I'm driving."

"And I'm coming too." Lav appears behind me. "For support," she twinkles innocently, and darts a look at Ro. Hmmm.

Mom waves us off, probably desperate for some peace and quiet, and we all wedge ourselves in Dad's car again. He delegates a separate responsibility to each of us to look behind, left, and right, since he doesn't have side mirrors anymore.

208

We drive to the conference center with only a couple of near misses (when Dad is changing lanes and the human side mirrors are checking Twitter).

The line looks even longer than last time. I dread to think how smelly the people are at the front of this one.

I feel the mood in the car sink a bit, so I give a little chirp on my whistle.

"Come on, team," I say cheerily, "third time lucky." We carefully unfold ourselves from the car, Roman and Lav with some reluctance. Honestly, between Mom and Dad and Lav and Roman, it is one big sex party around here.

We walk toward the entrance to the conference center, wondering if we have to line up again.

"Nah. They invited us," says Roman in reasonable tones. "Who invites a guest and then makes them line up at the front door?"

We hesitate a moment, then hear, "Hey! Guys?" from behind us—it's the security man from last time, the one who talked to his wrists. He was surly last time; this time he's practically *beaming*. Is he drunk? Does he think we're someone else?

"Morning, morning, morning!" He bounces up to us.

"*Hiiiii?*" we reply doubtfully.

"We *love* the video here," Wrists tells us. "Such big fans."

"Thanks!" I beam. Lav looks amused. Well, she's used to people sucking up to her. (I'm not, and it's *lovely*.)

"Have you seen all the remixes?" Wrists goes on. "I adore the track that Belgian DJ added to it. Is he a friend of yours?"

"I have no idea," I reply. *About anything you just said*, I want to add.

"Do you have representation?" he asks.

We look at each other, baffled.

"An agent? Or a manager?" he presses.

"Um, no, because what we do is we just sort of dance underwater in a community pool," says Gabe carefully.

"Should the kids go inside or speak to anyone?" asks Dad, making us sound like we've just turned up for a ten-year-old's party. Show biz!

Wrists leads us into the aircraft hangar. Immediately there's a camera in my face and a microphone even closer.

"Louise Brown, the Aquarium Boys' coach!" says a man I don't recognize. "We hear there was some police trouble after your video was shot. What was *that* all about?" he asks with a mischievous smile.

"Ah, well." I hesitate, sifting through all the insane details of that week and rejecting most of them as Too Harrowing for Chitchat.

Pete pulls me away by the arm and Dad, Lav, the Aquarium Boys, and I keep following Wrists. He leads us onto the stage. Lav and Dad hang back as we step in front of bright lights that blind us. We all blink and bump into each other. Wrists gives us a thumbs-up, then abandons us.

"Hello, guys!" comes a voice from the darkness out front.

"Hello . . . ?" we shout back doubtfully, shielding our eyes to see a table with three chairs behind it and a woman with an earpiece and a clipboard waving exaggeratedly at us.

"OK, guys, real quick," she says, ticking things off with her fingers as she goes through a list: "You'll be prepped at the side of stage." (What's prepping? *Will it hurt?*) "You'll come on, do your routine, *wait* for the judges to give you their feedback, then off. Quick off. It'll be *loud* in here with the audience—be prepared for that, and *do not* swear on camera."

"'Scuse me," I mumble. My mouth is dry and my tongue has gone big. *"Audienthe?"* I ask, but she's gone.

We all look at each other for a second until— "Clear the stage, please!" a voice booms from nowhere. Sorry, sorry, sorry.

We walk off, stand in the shadows with Dad and Laverne, and have a small nervous breakdown.

"This is not another public tryout," Pete says.

We all shake our heads silently.

"What?" says Lav.

"This is the televised audition," Ro says.

We nod. Lav's and Dad's eyes go big.

"That line," I say. They all look at me. "That line. It didn't have any ferrets in hats in it."

"Are you feeling all right, Lou?" Dad asks, feeling my forehead.

"You're right . . ." Gabe says faintly.

That gigantic line, snaking halfway around town, is not contestants but audience members.

chapter 34

Lou! We heard you guys are off to *BHT* today, that's beyond cool. Hook us up with some tickets? Ten should be fine. I'm having a party this weekend, sorry babes, forgot to invite you earlier, aargh, ditz! See you at *BHT*!

Imogen (Laverne's friend) xxxx

i know who Imogen is; she's acknowledged my existence *once* in six years. Twice now. I read her text and turn my phone off. I have more important things to worry about. We now have to wait three hours, which is really useful time in which to feel sick and pace around a lot. Roman nearly twists his ankle tripping on camera cables, so we force him to sit down. He can't get hurt. We're all out of substitutes now.

The term *dressing room* is too grand, but we definitely have a small room with no windows to ourselves. Plus there's a sign on the door that says *The Aquarium Boys*, and it's surrounded by stars. Gabe gets out his pen and changes it to *Lou Brown and the Aquarium Boys*.

Lav calls Mom to tell her "things have got a bit out of hand," which is one way of putting it. Mom and Hannah race along to join us, and Wrists brings them up to our room to wait with us. Roman and Gabe's parents are at work, and I think Pete is a little embarrassed about telling his dad. He just says, "Let's see how the day goes."

The mood in this room is like a shaken-up can of Coke. I try to calm them down. Coach to the rescue.

"Come on, guys, do some stretches, stay limber." The boys look at me, Gabe with a half smile, and I remember—I'm swimming too.

It's like someone just added Mentos to this can of Coke.

I step outside to use the bathroom, but really I just need a moment by myself to calm down. As I'm returning, I pass doors with signs like ours. Pete is loitering in the corridor. I realize he's waiting for me. He nods his head at one of the doors.

The sign says *Pretty in Sync*. I don't get it. He smirks and opens his mouth. Then the door opens and Nicole appears in the doorway.

"Oh!" She's surprised to see Pete, and I think I am literally invisible to her. "Pete Denners?" she says loudly, clearly meaning for everyone in the room to hear. "Are you waiting for Cammie?"

"Nope," he says honestly. "Bye, then!" He grabs me by the arm and rushes me back to our dressing room.

"But I thought she was sweet?" I tease him.

"Sweet like a *snake!*" he says. And maybe it's bitchy, but I'm glad the message got back to him.

Someone knocks on the door and we shuffle aside to let them in. Our visitors are three very pretty girls—who are very orange.

"Guys," one of them says, smiling, "we're here to give you a little makeup for the cameras." Her eyes roam over everyone in the room, resting hopefully on Lav.

"It's those three," says Gabe, pointing us out. The makeup artists hide their disappointment and set to work on our tired faces.

It's a strange feeling having little brushes dot and stroke my face. After about ten minutes my makeup artist steps back, satisfied, and I peek around her at the mirror. For the first time ever, I look like I might be related to Laverne.

My new vanity deflates with a farty sound as I notice that Roman and Pete are wearing more makeup than me and they look like supermodels. Sigh. This is the most beautiful I have *ever* looked, but still the boys are prettier.

Hannah catches my eye in the mirror. "You look amazing!" she mouths at me.

"You could look less surprised," I tell her sternly.

There's a sudden thundering of loud music from down the corridor.

"They're getting ready to begin," says my makeup artist, giving me a "Be brave" look. I give her a "Step Back Because I Might Be Sick on You" one in return. She steps back.

My face feels stiff with makeup. "Ank oo" is all I manage as the three girls wish us luck and leave.

I can tell I look scared, because Pete's being nice to me.

"We're going to be on in about an hour," he says gently, like I'm a dog waiting at the vet. "Do you want to watch the first part of the show from the side of the stage?"

We pad along the corridor, barefoot and wrapped in towels, with Gabe, Hannah, and my family in tow. I was sure I had mastered walking some years ago, but now my legs are all rubbery and they feel about eight feet long. We reach the backstage area, and the guys with earpieces wave us through. They seem to know who we are, which makes me feel a little better, because right now I don't think I can remember my surname. I haven't felt this nervous since the time trials.

Unhelpful memory. Shush shush shush, Lou.

And, unlike at the time trials, this time I have Mom, Dad, and Lav with me. The earpiece guys make way for us and point at a two-foot gap in the curtain where we can peek through and watch the show. We all step carefully, trying to not trip on all the stage equipment on the floor.

I bend down to put my face beneath Pete's; he moves the curtain so I can see. (*Stop being nice, it's freaking me out.*) There is a lady onstage who looks like someone's mom dancing around with a ribbon on a stick. I can't see the audience, but I can hear them openly laughing at her. I reel back slightly. What is *wrong* with people?

I hang back and find I'm next to Dad, who puts his arm around my shoulders and whispers in my ear, "You don't have to do this."

"I kind of *do*, though, don't I?" I whisper back.

"Well, yes," he admits, "but if you want to make a run for it, I'll go get the car."

We nod at each other. Deal.

The judges give their verdict on the woman and her ribbon, and they are brutal, saying the worst sort of YouTube comments, but to her face! I have a sudden urge to shower.

Next up, a father and son dressed as cows play pop songs on cowbells. Gabriel whispers in my ear, "Suddenly dancing under water feels normal." I smile at him, or I try to, but whatever they

215

sprayed on my face has left it rock hard and I wince and hold my cheek while he stifles a laugh. I haven't been this close to him since we were in Pete's Mini, and I wonder if he's thought about that since. I totally haven't. Nu-uh.

The act finishes and the father and son disappear off the other side of the stage. Now a huge tank is being lowered down in six pieces. The moment the first piece touches the floor, an army of people surge forward with tools to fit it all together. I watch them drag a hose onto the stage and start filling up the tank while they walk around checking all the joins and edges.

Soon the tank is in place, filled, and the show music booms to life. I hear the indistinct sound of the voice-over man announcing the start of the show, and the way he holds the last word for a long time, I can tell he's announced someone.

Hang on, what? Is it us now . . . ? They said we'd be fifteen minutes. Maybe I've lost track of time?

I throw off my towel and stumble forward. I have a terrifying moment of being blinded by the stage lights, and then someone pushes me firmly aside.

Debs is holding me back by the shoulder while her team sashays past, their faces lighting up with practiced plastic smiles the second they hit the stage. Cammie, Nicole, Amanda, and Melia—all in matching pink bathing suits.

For the first time all day I feel a real desperate desire to not do this, to just go home, put two chairs back to back, drape my duvet over them, and eat cheese on toast under there.

I don't even catch Debs's eye. I just walk away, back to my team, where Roman and Pete have grins on their faces. What are *they* so happy about? They'd better not still be excited about how "hot" Debs's team is. They lean toward me and take an ear each.

"You know her team already got through the tryouts weeks ago?" They tell me in stereo.

I nod.

Roman whispers gleefully, "Well we heard her freaking out, yelling at some poor guy backstage because now there are *two* swimming teams and only one can go through today."

He raises his eyebrows at me. Us! The thought that anyone might think me and my team could be equal with Debs's . . . I'm astonished.

Debs looks back at me and I can't stop myself—I give her my broadest smile. Which, thanks to the face spray, isn't very big, but she gets the idea and looks royally pissed off as she turns back to watch the stage.

We hear whooping and cheering from the audience.

"It sounds like they're doing well," says Pete nervously. Well, durr. He and Roman step forward to watch, but I grab them both by the elbows and shake my head.

"You swim no one's race but your own," I tell them firmly. They hesitate, but I know I'm right. I give them a "Listen to Coach" look and they do.

Because I am so wise *and* a massive hypocrite, I risk a peek when they're not looking. Debs's team is doing proper synchronized swimming. It looks good, really pro, perfectly in unison. Maybe I'm biased, but *I* think it's a little boring.

Our routine is more exciting: In some places it's *too* exciting and downright dangerous. Let's just hope the substitute doesn't ruin it all. I suddenly feel sick, and either my throat has got very small or the air here is too big.

Their routine comes to a triumphant end. I hear loud applause and then it quiets down, but I can't hear the judges' feedback, just the rumble of voices. I push my ear to the curtain and try to make out words, but I'm almost knocked off my feet by the team striding confidently backstage and waving over their shoulders at the audience.

Their jubilant mood doesn't last as Debs looms out of the darkness like a shark.

"*What* was that dive, Melia?"

Ugh, I think to myself, I do *not* miss that.

I look back and catch Hannah's eye, and she's clearly thinking the same thing. Debs doesn't even notice her one-time star swimmer standing in the shadows; she's too busy bullying her team all the way back to their dressing room. Like she used to do to me, back when she cared.

"OK," breathes Pete, interrupting my happy thoughts. "Show-time."

We snap our goggles into place. Gabriel holds out his arm and we give him our towels. I realize I'm still wearing the whistle, and after a moment's hesitation I take it off and place it around his neck.

"Good luck, Goldfish," he says, and kisses me on the cheek (but sort of near the mouth). I think that might technically count as my first kiss.

That is one impressively hot blush I have here. You could cook an egg on my head. Come on, Team, focus! (And yes, I've decided to start calling myself Team.)

The stagehands finish mopping up the water, the music starts again, and I hear the booming tones of the voice-over.

"Bwuuuur bwurrr BWWUUUURRRRR!" he shouts.

That's us, we're BWWUUUURRRR!

Roman strides out first, and I follow, Pete behind me. I feel calm all of a sudden. There's no point being scared; it is just going to happen now.

All my swimming training asserts itself and I start regulating my breathing.

You'd think it would feel weird being nearly naked in front of so many people, but it doesn't. I ping my swimsuit straps for luck, once right, twice left.

We climb the stairs up to the tank, and my knees shake with every step. My body feels unresponsive, as if I've borrowed it from someone for an hour. How do you *work* this thing? Where are the gears?

The three of us line up along the edge of the pool. I look down, then up, panicked—it's just a pool like last time—the sides are filled in! Please tell me this isn't going to happen to us again!

Six big men appear from the side of the stage and, in one dramatic move, pull away the plastic boards surrounding the pool. There's a *whoomph!* and lights shine through the water, dappling the faces of the judges and the audience with blue glimmerings. The lights move slowly, drifting past the tank—it's like they're recreating the acquarium video. Hope they didn't add an eel.

For the first time I catch a glimpse of the judges. I recognize them from the TV. There are two men and two women and they're all staring fixedly at us with slight frowns on their faces. What's this? they're thinking.

This is Lou Brown and the Aquarium Boys.

chapter 35

the music swells and fills the auditorium. We've spent weeks swimming to the music coming out of Lav's crappy little speaker dock, but this music is like a fireball hurling out from the stage. I can feel the bass vibrating in my ribs!

We raise our hands above our heads. There's a hushed silence as we wait for our cue. I can't begin to think about how many people are staring at us from the silent darkness behind the stage lights, so I fix my eyes on the water and visualize my dive.

Which is perfect. I feel the boys hit the water cleanly either side of me, and we corkscrew to the bottom, where everything is silent and calm.

We somersault backward in unison and I speed up as the others slow down. I watch the boys carefully out of the corner of my eye, then I rise up and they dive beneath me, push off from the bottom, hold a foot and a calf each and raise me into the air. I break the surface of the water and almost fall because I'm deafened by the roaring sound in the studio. Everyone is cheering!

The boys throw me up into the air and I somersault, knees tucked hard to my chest. I catch a quick glimpse of the judges' table before I dive down to the bottom and I'm back into the routine.

We swim around each other in a circle, then Pete peels off to lie on the floor of the pool, followed by me, then Roman. It sounds unspectacular, but it takes such control. You have to let all of the air out of your body, and we each exhale at a precise moment so that bubbles rush up from Pete, then me, then Roman. We slap our feet and upper arms on the bottom of the pool, push up hard, and kick with mermaid legs to reach the surface. By now we have no air left in our lungs and it takes a superhuman effort.

I always thought this would be the part that drowned Gabe. I'd watch him do this with my heart in my throat, poised to grab him and pull him out of the pool, but he always struggled through. It makes my head spin and my ears ring—that's why we put it at the end.

We lie on our backs on the surface of the pool like starfish, with our arms and legs interlocking. We need this bit to get our breath back for the final push, so as the music builds, we're panting and waiting for our cue. This is the moment where the bass swells, we thrust our arms above our heads, and dive backward underwater.

The routine ends with the three of us motionless.

Arms crossed over our chests.

Underwater.

Heads down.

Boom.

It gave *me* shivers watching the boys do that, through misted-up goggles in our school swimming pool with wart remover strips drifting past. It must look incredible now!

We surface and splash toward each other for a painfully hard group hug, which is a lot of slippery naked skin on skin.

We break apart prit-ty quick.

Gabe falls up the metal stairs to hug Roman, who pulls him into the water, and we're all hugging each other again. And then sinking, because that's how water works. And hugging and sinking again, because we're too excited to think straight. I can't believe we've actually done it! I don't even care what the judges thought!

Well . . . I do a little. So we swim to the edge of the pool, panting and pulling off our goggles. The judges are laughing and applauding, and the comedian is even wiping at his eyes.

"Well," says the mean one, spreading his hands wide as if he has no words, which makes the audience burst into roars and cheers again. It's deafening, actually painful to hear, but we're wincing and laughing.

"What even *is* that?" The pop star judge laughs and I shrug modestly like, "Just some new shizzle." We look at each other— we never really gave it a name, and I think if I said the words *synchronized* and *swimming* in front of everyone, Pete might push me out of the tank.

My hand slips off the edge of the pool and I put it back on again. But it slips off again and so does Gabe's. We glance at our hands, then each other, but the judges are still talking, so we try to focus on them. There's a ripple in the water, a strange *Jurassic Park*—style vibration that Roman and Pete don't seem to feel but Gabe and I do.

The surface of the water looks strange, and other people are beginning to notice it too. A couple of the stagehands walk briskly toward us, and the audience falls silent, confused.

Whenever I remember this bit later, it's always in slow motion.

Maybe it was so unexpected that that's the only speed I could process it at.

One side of this *massive* tank detaches and falls backward, off the stage.

I watch it fall with a dreamy indifference, and I'm vaguely aware of shouting, and someone grabs at my arms, but they can't hang on to me. My legs are cold and everything feels suddenly hazy.

The four of us lurch downward as the rest of the pool collapses and the water races toward the judges. Nothing feels like slow motion anymore. Gabe and I clutch hold of each other as the water throws us toward the judges' table and my head is submerged. Burning water shoots up my nose. I need to cough. I wrench my head upward, but there's just more water. Where *is* up? I can hear my heartbeat pounding in my ears, then people screaming, then heartbeat again as my head is ducked in and out of water.

There's a sharp pain in my lower back as I hit something—the table, a camera, a person . . . ? Gabe's hand slips from mine. I grab fruitlessly at nothing but can't find him again, and for the second time that month, I lose consciousness.

chapter 36

I wake up to bright lights, the rustle of crisp sheets, and a strangely familiar pressure on my chest. You only get tucked in this hard at the hospital.

It's a sign of an "interesting" life when you wake up in hospital so regularly that you can guess where you are with your eyes closed.

When I open them, Mom and Lav are sitting by the bed. Dad's in a chair in the corner—just like our last visit. But no one's crying this time.

They look delighted to see I'm awake and grin at me. The mood is definitely less serious. A nurse comes in to adjust my drip and check my charts. I think I recognize her from the last time.

Ugh, except this time it feels like I'm wearing a polo shirt made of cement. I'm in a neck brace and it's giving me an unfortunate double chin. I prop my jaw on the side, hoping that helps.

Lav gets to the point with characteristic gentleness. "Now that you're not dead, do you want the good news or the bad news?"

My throat hurts, so I hold up one finger, choosing option one.

"You nearly killed the judges of *BHT*."

I raise my eyebrows high.

She shrugs. "Well, I think they're annoying. I think it's a fine achievement."

"The boys are OK," says Dad. "You got the worst of it."

I roll my eyes. 'Course I did.

"Now get some rest," says Mom, putting a cool hand on my forehead. I turn my head to one side, trying to get comfortable, basking in the glow of our amazing performance. All that hard work, the nerves and the disasters, it was all worth it! We're TV stars.

I smile to myself, closing my eyes. I don't think I've ever been this happy. I'm a winner again— the Goldfish returns from the dead!

I have the unmistakable feeling I'm being watched. I open my eyes, and Mom, Dad, and Lav are all gathered tightly around my bed, looking at me. Dad brushes my hair back from my face. Aaah, love my family.

I close my eyes again.

I open them again. Family still clustered around my bed.

OK, gang. It's been emotional, but give a girl some *space*. How am I meant to have a nap while you're all gazing at me like I've just been born? Although I suppose I should get used to this; famous people have to put up with it all the time.

Imagine how everyone at school is going to act around me now? Cammie's gonna be gutted! Maybe Melia will finally get the guts to talk to me? Can't promise I'll be too excited. After all, I've got friends now, real friends.

Mom interrupts the little victory parade in my head.

"Lou. You were wonderful out there. It was a beautiful routine, wasn't it?" She turns to Dad and Lav.

"Amazing." Lav nods. "You're a choreographer!"

"Weirdest thing I've ever seen," says Dad honestly. "Don't know what goes on in that head of yours."

"We're all so proud of you." Mom smooths my hair behind my ear. "But you didn't get through to the next round."

I blink at her.

I think I must've gone temporarily insane. Because, and you'll laugh when I tell you, it's so ridiculous, but it *sounded* like she just said—

"You didn't go through. Debs's team did," says Lav, clearly going for the "rip the Band-Aid off quickly" approach.

"WHAT?" I croak. My jaw slips off the side of the neck brace.

"Darling," says Mom, "they couldn't use the footage."

"They think the damage to the stage, crew, and audience might run to six figures," Dad chips in.

"They might have to delay the next series because so many of the crew and judges are injured." Lav brings up the rear of the Bad News conga.

"I see. Anything else?"

"I got a parking ticket," Dad complains. "Which I'm appealing, because the sign said . . ." He subsides at a look from Lav. "Nothing else, that's all."

"Try to get some sleep," says Mom, and they all tiptoe out of the room to leave me "in peace." Aka to stew in my rage.

I spend the next few days in the hospital, having X-rays to check that I haven't chipped my spine or anything fun like that. Thankfully, I'm not the unluckiest person in the world, and I just have bruises.

After a day or so, Gabe hobbles in to see me with a sprained ankle and a bandage on his throat. He has a proud smile on his face and presents me with the sign from our dressing room: *Lou Brown and the Aquarium Boys.*

"Did they give you that?" I ask, delighted.

"Not exactly."

I turn the sign over and see large chips of paint on the back where he wrestled it off the door.

I examine the sign extremely carefully, suddenly a little shy. Gabe sits on my bed, but my bedsheets are tucked in so tightly that I'm pulled toward him until I'm lying on my side. We're very close now, and when I look up, his face is very near mine. And all I can think is, Beau Michaels tongue worms, Beau Michaels tongue worms.

Lav! She's psychologically scarred me before I got a chance to do any kissing of my own! I think angrily, but only for a second, because Gabe moves his face closer to mine and suddenly I *am* kissing. Gabe's lips are soft, and there is no darting tongue action at all. I feel smug. I'm clearly having better kissing than Lav was. I smell the sweet hair product from the aquarium and realize that was Gabe, not Roman.

We're holding hands while we kiss, but as he moves closer, we break away, laughing. I don't know if you've ever tried to hug someone with a large cardboard sign in between you, but it's difficult, risky work. We break apart, ruefully rubbing our chins where the sign poked us.

"When you get out of the hospital, would you like to do something?" he asks.

"Do? Like a new swim team?" I ask, just in case he doesn't mean a date. I don't want to embarrass myself.

"No, like do something like a date!" he exclaims, rolling his eyes.

227

(*He did mean do something like a date*! I sing inside.)

"Cool, sure, whev." I shrug. "I'm pretty chill about it, but if I have time, you know . . ."

Gabe gets up and props my sign on my windowsill where I can see it. "Go to sleep, you're very annoying," he says, and kisses me on the cheek.

He leaves, but I don't go to sleep. I just lie there, looking at my sign

After a while I get a stiff neck, so I turn my head toward the door. There's a little plastic bag sitting in the doorway like a visitor. I get up to investigate, but Nurse Juliet notices and runs at me, hissing "Bed rest!" so I clamber back into bed. She hands me the bag, and when I root through it, I find ten new pairs of underwear. I did need new underwear, but not mysterious ones.

Hmm. Either

a) I have a secret admirer who's weird but helpful,
b) I've had a visit from the Underwear Fairy,
c) or they're magic and I've got a place at Hogwarts.

Gabe comes back a few hours later with Pete (broken fingers), Roman (bruised ribs, cut legs), and Lav (absolutely fine.) The boys weren't on bed rest, so they've been more active than me and have been picking up all the news that we missed after we DE-STROYED *Britain's Hidden Talent*.

Pete is very excited. "So apparently, while there's no chance we'll make it onto the show because the studio cameras got water damage, tons of people filmed us on their phones and put the videos on YouTube, where the views have already overtaken our first video!"

Ro is adamant that this is way better than being on the show, because we get all the fame but also a kind of underground edgy vibe. Good, I'm glad, I say vaguely, that's exactly the sort of vibe I've always wanted.

I'm distracted—Lav is sitting a *little* too close to Roman on my bed. I give her a narrowed-eyes look.

Later, when the boys leave, she preempts me—"But he's so lovely!"

"I know!" I say. "That's why you'd better be nice to him."

"He was so worried about you. He wouldn't get in the ambulance until he saw you were OK."

That is very sweet. And I'm happy for the two of them. I wonder if Ro does the tongue worm thing? I smirk to myself. It'd be funny if Lav got the bad kisser out of the family and I got the good one. Rude to brag about, though.

Lav hops off the bed to leave. "Did you get the bag of underwear I left you?" she asks.

The smirk droops on my face. "Uh. Yes, thank you," I reply, smoothing my blanket and avoiding eye contact. "When did you leave it there, out of interest?"

Lav checks her watch. "I'm not sure. What time did you start kissing Gabe? I got here about a second before that."

I stare at the duvet, feeling the blood rush to my ears.

"Thank you for stopping by, Laverne."

"Is he your boyfriend?"

"Please go, I'm very ill, I need my rest."

"This is adorable. *Gabe!*"

I put my head under the pillow until my ears cool down.

the end 2

i race toward an unfamiliar sports center, taking the steps two at a time.

"Come *on*!" I yell over my shoulder.

I run inside and look frantically around. Ah, that way! I look back and point. "I'm going this way, come on!"

Gabe staggers through the door after me, panting. "Yelling 'come on' doesn't make my legs longer. If it did, I'd shout at them too."

I feel a stab of guilt and maybe love (or a stitch). I grab his bag from him to lighten his load.

"I can carry you if you're tired."

"Shut up and keep moving."

We had to take three buses to get here. We've been rushing for about two hours and we're *still* late. The chlorine smell is getting stronger as we power walk along the corridor, and I push through a set of heavy doors to find myself in the viewing gallery of a huge glass-roofed space with four swimming pools in it.

I flop down on a bench and start scanning the swimmers for a familiar face. A second later Gabe lands beside me with a thud. We both glow with sweaty heat. Gabe pulls off his sweater. I don't, not yet.

"I'm glad your dad got a job," he grumbles, his sweater halfway over his head, "but I do miss the free taxi service."

"The food's gone downhill too," I tell him. "Mom fried pasta leftovers the other day. Oh!" I spot her and pinch Gabe accidentally hard.

"Ow! Good!" He rubs his arm and we both wave.

Hannah is standing by the side of the blocks, getting ready for her race. I'm so glad we made it in time. I wave frantically to get her attention. The family behind me tuts, but I don't care. She spots me and gives me an aggressive thumbs-ups in return.

I unzip my hoodie to reveal my T-shirt.

It's bespoke. (Up yours, Debs.) It's got a giant photo of Hannah's sleeping face on it—I stand up and point at it. She looks subtly delighted. To the untrained eye she looks annoyed and embarrased.

I settle down next to Gabe and we lean forward, watching intently, no more joking around. Hannah's competing to get into the High Performance Training Camp again. I know she can make the times, and she'll deal better with the pressure this time. Especially since she had a Firm Word with her parents.

I see Debs talking to her. She's coaching her again. Hannah nods, listening. Debs's team, Pretty in Sync, made the semifinals of *Britain's Hidden Talent*. When they were eliminated before the final, Debs stormed the stage and had to be dragged off the judges' table by security. She became briefly notorious.

I think public shame has been good for her. Character building or something. All I know is, I loved it. I watched that video a *lot* on-line. Along with lots of other people.

Hannah gets up on her block; the room calms down. Hannah stops looking at the other swimmers now. She looks straight ahead. You swim no one's race but your own.

I hope she knows that if she hates the camp this time around, I'm always available for prison breaks.

She bends and wraps her fingers around the edge of the block. There's a pause, then the starting pistol bangs, and she dives, hard.

I watch Hannah, and Gabe watches me. I feel his eyes on me and I smile and grab his hand. I'm swimming my own race.

acknowledgments

Thanks Mum and Dad! Top billing for long service.

Thanks to my tenacious and brilliant agent, Hellie Ogden at Janklow and Nesbit—for finding me in the aftermath of disaster and insisting that NOW was the perfect time to write this book. You were right, you're always right!

The original Lou— Lu Corfield, for letting me live and write in your house when I had nowhere to live! (This happens to me far too often. Must concentrate.)

My wonderful UK editor, Emma Lidbury at Walker, for her support, encouragement and—most important—great notes. Thanks for your patience with my chronology, sometimes in Lou's world it's always Tuesday and then we lose a month. No one knows why.

Love and thanks to Walker Books, which is exactly the sort of place you imagine the books get made. And where everyone is always welcoming even when I'm annoying Jack Noel about the cover and stealing books.

I'm very grateful to Jessica Fullalove, an awesome British swimmer who patiently answered all my divvy questions about her job.

I'm very excited to be published by Macmillan in America, thank you so much Jean Feiwel for making that happen, Anna Booth for the awesome cover design, and Anna Roberto for ensuring that Lou makes sense when she travels! The whole pants/pants thing was a minefield.

Thank you to my European publishers—Gallimard Jeunesse in France, cbt Verlag in Germany and Piemme in Italy—I'm delighted that Lou is becoming more well-travelled than me! And to Rebecca Folland and Kirsty Gordon at Janklow and Nesbit for all their skill and patience. International tax is a world of pain that I won't ever understand but hey, at least we TRIED? (If HMRC is reading this . . . I swear—I paid.)